Fierce and Gentle Warriors

Fierce and Gentle Warriors

Three Stories by

Mikhail Sholokhov

TRANSLATED BY MIRIAM MORTON

ILLUSTRATED BY MILTON GLASER

DOUBLEDAY & COMPANY, INC.

GARDEN CITY, NEW YORK, 1967

Contents

Introduction

Mikhail sholokhov is a Russian author whose works are identified with life on the River Don and on the immense steppes through which it flows. This is borne out in the very title of the epic novel which won for Sholokhov, in 1965, the Nobel Prize for Literature—*And Quiet Flows the Don*.

The Don may have flowed quietly, but not so the human life around it. The stories offered in this volume, as much as his longer writings, show how life on the Don had been deeply shaken by the tempests of the times which they tell about. The lives of the Don people, grown-ups and children, were dramatically caught in the violent currents of the 1917 Revolution, the Civil War, and the Second World War.

To understand and enjoy Sholokhov's stories, it is important to know something about the history of the Don region and its inhabitants, the Cossacks.

This part of Russia was, for several centuries, the equivalent of the American Wild West. The Don region's rich soil, vast virgin lands, opportunities for independence and adventure, and possibilities for greater personal freedom, had lured men who were at odds with the authorities and with their masters. Many thousands fled to the Don from the more tame, repressive, poverty-stricken, often utterly hopeless existence they had led elsewhere in Czarist Russia.

Here, therefore, had come despairing slaves, wanderers, runaway soldiers, fugitives, bandits, rebels. This mixture of uprooted men craving a new life had taken on, with time, the character of a fiercely independent and violent people. Circumstances too involved to describe here had turned them into a population of warrior-peasants. Such were the Cossacks. And the ways of these people have remained different even to this day, despite the fact that they have been absorbed into the mainstream of Soviet life.

Mikhail Sholokhov is himself a Cossack. He was born in 1905 in a small village on the Don. Except for three of his sixty years, spent in Moscow, he has lived, farmed, and evolved into a major writer in this same Cossack village. He lives there now.

The Revolution of 1917 and the Civil War that followed disrupted his life and interrupted his schooling. Sholokhov never resumed his formal education after the age of thirteen. When still in his early teens, and during the entire four years of the Civil War, he fought with the Red forces of Don peasants against bands of White Cossacks. These "Whites" were brutally opposed to the new order ushered in by the Revolution. They stopped at nothing in their determination to restore the power of the Czar and to return the landless Cossack peasant to his former state of dependence and poverty. The Reds fought back with equal relentlessness.

Sholokhov was eighteen when this struggle ended. He spent the next three years in Moscow, working as a bricklayer and stevedore, and trying to become a writer.

His first stories were published during those three years. *The Rascal* (1925) and *The Colt* (1926), in this volume, are among these early stories.

In all of his writings Sholokhov reveals the contrasting traits of toughness and gentleness. The toughness and the gentleness appear differently in each of the three stories offered in this volume. We also find in them all the other qualities in Sholokhov's work that have impressed readers, critics, and fellow writers. We find in them his forceful realism, the vivid detail, the manly warmth of heart, and the wry humor.

Sholokhov has written only about people and events intimately known to him. His characters and the events in which they are involved are therefore completely believable—their violence, their outrage, their courage, their heartbreak, and their laughter.

The Fate of a Man, the third story in this volume, was first published in 1957, more than thirty years after *The Rascal* and

The Colt. We find in this moving story about an ordinary soldier in the war against the Nazis, the same admiration for the heroism of the ordinary man, the same tender feeling for the young creature or child who is the innocent victim of violence and destruction, the same awareness of the healing powers of nature in the midst of havoc. But we also find in it even a greater mastery in revealing the deepest feelings of his characters. This story gives an unforgettable portrayal of the capacity of man to respond with courage, loyalty, and love in the face of desperate circumstances.

In announcing the award of the Nobel Prize for Literature to this author, the Swedish Academy stated that he was thus honored for "the artistic power and integrity" of his epic work, *And Quiet Flows the Don.* The stories in this volume are marked with the same artistic power and integrity.

MIRIAM MORTON

Fierce and Gentle Warriors

The Colt

HE STRUGGLED out of his mother's body in broad daylight, head first. His spindly front legs stretched out near a pile of manure buzzing with emerald flies, and the first thing he saw was the dove-gray puff of a shrapnel explosion melting overhead. The roar of a cannon split the air and threw his little wet body under his mother's legs. Terror was the first feeling he knew on this earth.

An ill-smelling hail of grapeshot rattled on the tiled roof of the stable and sprinkled the ground below. The frightened mother jumped to her feet and with a shrill neigh dropped down again, her sweating flank resting against the sheltering dung heap.

She was soldier Trofim's mare.

In the sultry silence that followed, the buzzing of the flies could be heard more clearly. A rooster, scared by the gunfire and not daring to jump to the top of the fence, flapped his wings several times somewhere in the safety of the bushes, and crowed there with abandon. From the hut came the tearful groans of a wounded machine-gunner. He cried out repeatedly in a voice sharp yet hoarse, and his cries were mingled with fierce oaths. Bees were humming among the silky heads of the poppies in the small garden. Beyond the village a machine gun was finishing off its belt, and to the rhythm of its weirdly cheerful chatter, in the interval between the cannon shots, the mare lovingly licked her firstborn. And the colt, lowering himself to his mother's swollen

13

udder, sensed for the first time the fullness of life and the unforgettable sweetness of a mother's caresses.

After the second shell had crashed somewhere behind the barn, Trofim emerged from the hut, slammed the door, and walked toward the stable. As he was passing the manure pile, he shielded his eyes from the sun with the palm of his hand and, seeing the colt quiver with the strain of sucking at his mare, he was spellbound and dumfounded. With trembling hands he fumbled for his tobacco pouch. After rolling himself a cigarette, he regained his power of speech:

"So-o-o! I see you've gone and foaled! You've picked a fine time, I must say!" There was a bitter note of injury in his last remark.

Scrub grass and dry dung clung to the mare's shaggy flanks. She looked indecently thin and loose, but her eyes beamed with a proud joy touched with weariness, and her satany upper lip curled back in a grin. Or so at least it seemed to Trofim. He led his mare into the stable. She snorted as she shook the bag of grain he hung from her head. Trofim leaned against the doorpost and, looking crossly at the colt, asked his mother dryly:

"What the devil am I going to do with him?"

The sound of grain being crunched could be heard in the dimness and stillness of the stable. A crooked sunbeam, like a column of golden dust, shed its light through a chink in the closed door and shone on Trofim's cheek. His whiskers and the brush of his beard were tinged with a reddish hue. The lines around his mouth curved in dark furrows. The colt stood on its thin, downy legs like a wooden toy horse.

"Will I have to kill him?" Trofim said, pointing his tobacco-stained forefinger in the direction of the newborn.

The mare rolled her bloodshot eyeballs, blinked, and gave her master a sidelong, mocking glance.

That evening, inside the best room of the hut, Trofim had a conversation with the Squadron Commander:

". . . I could tell my mare was in foal, she couldn't trot, I couldn't get her to canter, and she kept getting short of breath. I had taken a good look at her one day and it turned out she was in foal. And what care she took of it! Such care! You know, the colt is a sort of bay color . . . That's how . . ." Trofim told his story, hesitating between the details.

The Squadron Commander clutched the copper mug of tea in his fist as he would clutch a sabre hilt before going into battle, and kept staring at the lamp with tired eyes. Above the yellow flame moths flew about in a frenzy. They had flown in through the open window and were burning themselves against the lamp's glass chimney, one after another.

"It makes no difference—bay or black—it's all the same. Shoot it! With a colt around we'll be like a gypsy camp, not a cavalry squadron," the Commander said.

Trofim muttered something.

"What? . . . That's what I said, just like gypsies. And if the Chief were to show up, what then? There he'll be, reviewing the regiment, and the colt will come prancing out with its tail up. . . . The whole Red Army will be shamed and disgraced. I don't understand how you could have allowed such a thing, Trofim. Here we are, at the very height of the Civil War, and suddenly, there is this kind of thing going on. Why, it's downright disgraceful! Give the hostlers the strictest orders to keep the stallions away from the mares."

Next morning Trofim came out of the hut carrying his rifle. The sun hadn't yet fully risen. The grass was sparkling with roseate dew. The meadow, marked with traces of the infantry's boots and dug up for trenches, reminded one of a girl's tear-stained, sorrowful face. The cooks were bustling around the field kitchen. On the porch of the hut the Commander was sitting in a threadbare undershirt. As he sat there, shaping a ladle out of wood, his fingers, now more

15

accustomed to the chilly touch of a revolver, were awkward at this task. The feel and fragrance of the damp wood brought back to him the forgotten past of village life.

As Trofim went by he asked, with a show of interest:

"Making a dumpling ladle?"

The Commander finished off the handle and said through his teeth:

"That woman, that pest of a housekeeper, kept after me: 'Do, please make me one. . . .' At one time I was good at this sort of thing, but now somehow it doesn't come out right."

"No, on the contrary . . . I think it's quite good," Trofim praised his Commander's handiwork.

He brushed the chips off his knees and asked Trofim:

"Going to shoot the colt?"

Trofim waved his hand and said nothing. After a moment's pause he walked on toward the stable.

With head bent, the Commander waited for the sound of the shot. A minute passed, then another, but he heard nothing. Trofim reappeared from around the corner of the stable. He looked distressed.

"Well?"

"Something must be wrong with the hammer of the rifle. It won't strike the percussion cap."

"Let me have a look at it."

Trofim reluctantly handed over his rifle. The Commander pulled the bolt back and forth, and screwed up his eyes.

"You have no bullets in it."

"Can't be!" Trofim exclaimed.

"I tell you it's empty."

"Guess I must have dropped them somewhere . . . maybe behind the stable."

The Commander laid the rifle aside and spent some time turning over the new ladle in his hands. The scent of the moist wood was so strong that his nostrils quickened to the fragrance of flowering alders and of newly plowed earth. He

16

thought longingly of past toil almost forgotten in the endless conflagration of war.

"All right! The devil with him! Let him stay near his mother. For the time being let him live . . . then we'll see. When the war is over, he may yet be of some use—maybe for plowing. . . . And if anything goes wrong, the Chief will understand that the colt is a suckling and must be allowed to nurse . . . the Chief was once a suckling himself . . . and we have nursed too . . . and since it is the way of nature, that's all there is to it! But, there's nothing whatever wrong with your rifle."

It so happened that a month later, not far from the village of Ust-Khopersk, Trofim's squadron was engaged in battle with a company of enemy Cossacks. The two sides opened fire at twilight. It was getting dark as they rode into attack, sabres bared. Halfway in the charge Trofim had fallen behind his platoon. Neither the whip nor the bit, which Trofim pulled so hard that his mare's mouth bled, could get her to break into a gallop. Tossing her head high, she neighed hoarsely and stamped the ground until the colt, waving his tail, caught up with her. Trofim leaped from his saddle, thrust his sabre into its scabbard, and, his face contorted with rage, tore the rifle from his shoulder. The men on the right flank were already in hand-to-hand combat with the enemy. Near a cliff a group of fighters was moving back and forth as if swayed by a strong wind. They brandished their sabres in silence. Only the dull thud of the horses' hoofs could be heard. Trofim glanced in their direction for a second, then aimed at the colt's narrow head. His hand may have trembled in his exasperation, or perhaps there was some other reason for it, but he missed his aim. After the shot the colt merely kicked up his heels stupidly, neighed in a thin voice and, throwing up clumps of gray dirt, circled around and came to a standstill a little way off. Trofim fired several more bullets at the little devil. Then, convinced that the

17

shots had caused neither injury nor the death of his mare's offspring, he leaped on to her back, and swearing monstrously, rode off at a jogtrot to where bearded, red-faced Cossacks were pressing his Squadron Commander and three other Red Army men toward a gully.

The squadron spent that night in the steppe, near a shallow gully. The men smoked little. They didn't unsaddle the horses. A reconnaissance returning from the Don reported that considerable enemy forces had gathered to prevent the Reds from crossing the river.

As Trofim lay dozing, his feet wrapped in the folds of a rubber cloak, he could not stop thinking of the events of the past day.

Before dawn, the Commander came over and squatted down beside him in the darkness.

"Trofim, are you asleep?"

"Just dozing."

Looking up at the fading stars, the Commander said:

"Get rid of that colt. He's causing trouble in battle. When I look at him my hand shakes. . . . I can't use my sabre. It's all because he reminds us of home . . . and we can't have that sort of thing in war . . . it turns the soldier's heart from stone to a limp rag. And, besides, when the horses went into attack the scamp got between their legs and they wouldn't tread on him." The Commander was silent a moment, then smiled sadly. But Trofim did not see the smile. "Do you understand, Trofim?" he continued. "That colt's tail . . . seeing that tail . . . the way he puts it over his back, kicks up his heels . . . and his tail is just like a fox's. . . . It's a marvelous tail! . . ."

Trofim remained silent. He drew his coat over his head and, shivering in the dewey dampness, fell asleep with astonishing speed.

Opposite a certain ancient monastery, the Don strikes against projecting cliffs and dashes past them with reckless swiftness. At the bend the water spins in little whirlpools, and the green, white-maned waves rush to fling themselves against the chalk rocks scattered into the river by the spring floods.

The enemy had occupied the shore where the current was weaker and the river broader and calmer. They were on the right bank. They were now aiming their fire at the foot-hills across from their vantage point. To avoid the line of fire, the Squadron Commander could not do otherwise than have his men cross the rushing river opposite the monastery. He rode down from the sandbank beneath the cliffs and led the way into the water with his bay horse. The rest of the squadron followed him with a thunderous splash—one hundred and eight half-naked swimmers and the same number of horses of varied colors. The saddles were piled into three canoes. Trofim was steering one of them. He had entrusted his mare to the platoon leader, Nechepurenko. From the middle of the river Trofim could see the leading horses wading deeply, forced to gulp water. Their riders urged them on. In less than a minute, some one hundred and fifty feet from the shore, the water was thickly dotted with horses' heads, snorting in a variety of sounds. The men swam at their sides, clinging to their manes, clothes and knapsacks tied to rifles which they held above their heads.

Throwing his oar into the boat, Trofim rose to his full height and, screwing up his eyes against the sun, looked anxiously for his mare's head among the swimming horses. The squadron resembled a gaggle of geese scattered over the sky by hunters' shots. Right in front was the Squadron Commander's bay, his glossy back rising high out of the water. Behind it was a dark cloud of animals and, last of all, falling more and more behind the others, as Trofim could see, came platoon leader Nechepurenko's bristling head, with the pointed ears of Trofim's mare on his left. Straining his eyes,

21

Trofim also caught sight of the colt. He was swimming in spurts, rising high out of the water, then sinking till his nostrils were barely visible.

And then the wind passing over the Don carried to Trofim's ears a plaintive neigh, as thin as a spider's thread.

The cry sounded over the water as sharp and keen as the point of a sabre. It struck right at Trofim's heart, and something extraordinary happened to the man: he had gone through five years of war, death had gazed like a temptress into his eyes again and again, and who knows what else. But now he went pale under his red bushy beard, turning the color of ashes. Snatching up the oar, he sent the boat back against the current, toward the spot where the exhausted colt was spinning in a whirlpool. And some sixty feet away, Nechepurenko was struggling with the mare but could not hold her back. She was swimming toward that whirlpool, whinnying in distress. Trofim's friend, Steshka Yefremov, sitting on a pile of saddles in another canoe, shouted to him:

"Don't take a fool's chances. Make for the shore. Look! There they are—the Cossacks!"

"I'll shoot him!" Trofim cried, his breath coming hard as he tugged at his rifle strap.

The current had carried the colt to where the squadron was crossing. The small whirlpool swung him around and around smoothly, lapping against him with its green, foam-capped waves. Trofim worked his oar desperately as the boat lurched violently. He could see the Cossacks rushing out of a ravine on the right shore. A Maxim gun began its rapid drumming. The bullets hissed as they smacked into the water. An enemy officer in a torn canvas shirt shouted something, waving his rifle.

The colt whinnied more and more rarely, the short, piercing cry grew fainter and fainter. And that cry sounded so much like the cry of an infant that it sent a chill of horror through all who heard it.

24

Nechepurenko, abandoning the mare, easily swam back to the left shore. Trembling, Trofim seized his rifle and fired, aiming just below the small head being sucked down by the whirlpool. Then he kicked off his boots and, stretching out his arms dived into the river with a dull moan.

On the right bank the officer in the canvas shirt bellowed: "Cease fire!"

Within five minutes Trofim reached the colt. With his left hand he supported his chilled body, and panting and coughing in spasms, made for the left shore. Not a shot was fired from the opposite side.

Sky, forest, sand—all glowingly green, transparent. . . . With one last tremendous effort Trofim's feet felt the ground. He dragged the colt's slippery body onto the shore, and, sobbing, spat up the green water as he groped over the sand with his hands. From the forest across the Don came the muffled voices of his squadron that had made the crossing. Somewhere beyond the sandbank on the opposite side rifle shots rang out. The mare stood at Trofim's side, shaking herself and licking her colt. From her tail a rainbow stream was dripping, making small holes in the sand.

Swaying, Trofim rose to his feet, took a few steps, then sprang into the air and dropped on his side. He felt as though a hot arrow had pierced his chest. He heard the shot as he fell. A single shot in the back, from the opposite shore. There the officer in the torn canvas shirt casually rattled his carbine lock ejecting the smoking cartridge case, while on the sand, two paces from the colt, Trofim twitched and his rough blue lips, which for five years had not kissed a child, smiled for the last time.

1926

The Rascal

I

M ishka was dreaming that his grandfather had cut down a long, thick cherry switch in the garden and was coming after him, waving the switch and saying threateningly:

"Come over here, Mikhail Fomich—I'm going to warm up the place your legs grow out of, for you."

"What did I do?" Mishka asked.

"You stole all the eggs from under the speckled hen and swapped them for rides on the merry-go-round. That's what you did, you squirt."

"But Grandpa, I haven't had a single ride on the merry-go-round this whole year," Mishka shouted in alarm.

"Bend over, you rascal, and pull down your pants."

Mishka cried out and woke up. His heart was pounding as if he had really had a taste of that switch. He opened his left eye the tiniest bit and saw it was daylight in the family hut. Through the small window he could see the dawn warming up. Mishka raised his head and heard voices out on the porch. His mother was chattering away about something, crying and laughing at the same time, and his grandfather was coughing, while a strange voice was saying something that sounded like "Boo-boo-boom."

Mishka rubbed his eyes as he saw the door opening and slamming shut again, then his grandfather running into the best room and standing there bobbing up and down, his glasses bouncing about on his nose. At first Mishka thought

27

the priest had come with his singers—his grandfather had bustled about happily like that when they had come at Easter time. But following the old man a huge soldier in an overcoat and a cap with no peak, pushed his way into the best room, while Mishka's mother hung on this big man's neck, sobbing away.

In the middle of the hut the stranger stopped, freed himself from her hold and shouted:

"Where's my heir?"

Mishka panicked and dived under the quilt.

"Minuyshka, wake up, sonny, your dad is home from the front!" his mother cried.

Before Mishka had time to blink, the soldier grabbed him, threw him up to the ceiling, then hugged him hard and started in earnest to prick him with his red whiskers on his lips, cheeks, and even his eyelids. And his whiskers were wet with something salty. Mishka tried to tear himself away but it was no use.

"He's grown into a fine specimen! Will soon outgrow his old man! Ho-ho-ho!" his father roared and began to toss Mishka about like a feather, balancing him on his palm, twirling him around, and throwing him up again and again to the highest beam in the ceiling.

Mishka put up with all this nonsense for a while, then he puckered his brows sternly, like his grandfather when he meant business, pulled hard on his father's whiskers, and commanded:

"Let me go, Dad!"

"No, I won't let you go."

"Let me go! I'm big now and you're playing with me like with a baby."

His father seated Mishka on his knee, and asked with a smile:

"How old are you, big shot?"

"I'm seven," Mishka muttered, scowling at his father.

"Is that so? And do you still remember, sonny, how I

made boats for you two years ago, and how we sailed them on the pond?"

"I remember," Mishka said after thinking a while, and shyly put his arms around his father's neck.

And then the celebrating really began. His father put Mishka on his shoulders, and holding him by the legs went galloping around the room, bucking and neighing just like a horse, until Mishka almost lost his breath screaming with delight. His mother pulled at his sleeve and yelled:

"Come on, go outside and play, you screaming monkey!" And to Mishka's father she complained: "Let him go, Foma. Please let him go. He doesn't give me a chance to even look at you, my shining eagle. I haven't set eyes on you for two years, and now he's all you can think of."

He put Mishka down and said:

"Run along and play with the boys for a while. When you come back I'll show you what I've brought you."

Mishka went out, closed the door behind him, and thought at first of standing there and listening to what the grownups had to say inside. But then he remembered that none of the kids knew yet that his father had come home and he ran across his yard, dashed over the vegetable garden treading down the holes made ready for the potato planting, and flew toward the pond.

He went swimming in the smelly, stagnant water, rolled over in the sand, had one last dive, and hopping on one foot, pulled on his pants. He was about to run home when Vitka, the priest's son, appeared.

"Don't go yet, Mishka. Let me have a swim. Then you come to my place to play. Your mother said it was all right for you to come to my house."

Mishka held up his falling pants with his left hand, pulled up his suspenders with the other, and said indifferently:

"I don't care to play with you. You have something smelly coming out of your ears."

Vitka screwed up one eye spitefully and said as he pulled his shirt off his scrawny shoulders:

"That's because of scrofula, but you, you're just a peasant."

"Is that so?"

"I heard our cook tell my mother."

Mishka dug at the sand with his foot and looked Vitka up and down.

"My daddy fought in the war, but your daddy doesn't work and he eats other people's pies."

"You're a rotten louse," the priest's son shouted, curling his lip scornfully.

Mishka snatched up a stone. Vitka held back his tears and smiled sweetly:

"Don't hit me, Mishka. Don't be mad at me. Here, do you want it?—you can have my dagger—it's made of iron."

"My dad brought me one back from the war that's better than yours."

"That's a lie!" Vitka said unconvinced.

"You're a liar yourself! When I say he did, he did. And he brought me a real rifle, too."

"My, haven't you become rich all of a sudden?" Vitka mocked with envy.

"And he also has an army cap."

Vitka thought hard how to impress Mishka, wrinkling his forehead and scratching his stomach.

"And my daddy will soon be a bishop, and yours was a cowherd, so there!"

By now Mishka had had enough of standing there arguing, he turned his back on Vitka and walked away toward the orchard. The priest's son called after him:

"Mishka, Mishka, I have something to tell you."

"Go ahead, tell me."

"Come nearer."

Mishka turned back, stood closer to Vitka, and looked at him suspiciously.

"Well?"

Vitka began to jump up and down on his thin, crooked legs, grinning and shouting:

"Your father is a dirty Communist, and when you die your soul will fly up to heaven, but God will say: 'Because your father was a Red you go down to hell.' And down there the devils will start roasting you in a frying pan, and they'll roast you and roast you."

"And how about you? Aren't they going to roast you?"

"My daddy's a priest, but you're an ignorant good-for-nothing and you don't understand anything."

Mishka was too scared of those devils to say any more. He turned and ran home.

Feeling somehow safer by the time he reached the orchard fence, he turned around, shook his fist at Vitka, and said:

"I'm going to ask my grandfather about the frying pan. If you were lying, don't you dare come into our yard!"

He climbed over the fence and ran toward his hut, seeing before his eyes the frying pan with himself, Mishka, in it being fried. It was burning hot there and the fat was spluttering and bubbling. Shivers ran up and down his back. He could hardly wait to get to his grandfather and ask him.

As bad luck would have it, the sow got in his way. It had got stuck in the narrow wicket gate, its head outside, its body in the yard, with its feet dug into the ground, and the tail wiggling away. It was squealing piercingly. Mishka set about freeing the prisoner. He tried to open the gate wider, but the sow began to wheeze. He then sat astride on her back and pulled. The pig strained and strained, tore off the gate, shrieked as if it was being butchered, and took off toward the barn, Mishka riding her, his heels banging against her sides to make her go faster. And they were speeding at such a pace that Mishka's hair stood on end as if blown by the wind. He jumped off at the barn, looked around, and saw his grandfather standing on the porch beckoning to him with his finger.

"Come here, my dove."

31

Mishka didn't suspect why his grandfather was calling him, but he remembered all at once about that frying pan in hell and ran toward the old man.

"Grandpa, Grandpa, are there devils somewhere in the sky?"

"I'll give you devils right here and now. I'll spit on a certain place and then dry it off with the switch. You evil brat, why were you riding that pig?"

He seized Mishka by the forelock and called his mother out from the best room.

"Come and admire your smart son."

She came running.

"What has he done now?"

"What has he done?! I just saw him riding the pig so fast that the dust flew under them."

"Not the sow that's going to farrow?!" the mother groaned.

Before Mishka could open his mouth to explain, his grandfather pulled the leather belt from his waist and, holding up his trousers with his other hand, pushed Mishka's head between his knees and began to whack him, saying wrathfully with each stroke:

"You're not to ride on the pig, you're not to ride on the pig!"

Mishka started to wail, and the old man added:

"You scoundrel, don't you even have pity on your own father? He's dead tired from his trip home and lay down to have a sleep, and you raise a howl."

So what could Mishka do?—he had to keep quiet. He tried to kick his grandfather, that wouldn't have made much noise, but he couldn't get at him. His mother grabbed him and pushed him into the hut.

"You sit there, you little devil. You'll get it later."

The grandfather sat on the bench in the kitchen, now and then looking at Mishka's back.

Mishka turned around toward him, smeared the last tear with his fist, and said:

"You just wait. . . ."

"Are you threatening your own grandfather, you evil child?"

Mishka saw the old man unfastening his belt again and quickly slipped off his seat, opened the door a little ways, just in case, and watching his every move, went on:

"You just wait, just wait, Grandpa dear—when all your teeth fall out I won't even chew for you. Don't even bother to ask me." Mishka banged the door and fled.

His grandfather walked out on the porch and saw his grandson's golden head diving in and out of the tall green shaggy hemp bushes as he sped through the garden, and his blue pants flashing in the sunlight. The old man stood there threatening him with his stick and trying to bury his smile in his beard.

II

To his father he was Minka. To his mother Minuyshka. To his grandfather, in his loving moments, he was a wicked little rascal, and at other times, when his eyebrows descended in gray tufts over his angry eyes, it was: "Hey, Mikhail Fomich, come over here. I'll warm your ears for you."

But to the rest, to the gossips, to the kids, to the entire village, he was Mishka and "the shame-child."

His mother had given birth to him before she was wed. And although she married the herdsman, Foma, by whom she had had her son, a month later, the nickname "shame-child" had stuck to Mishka like a sore, and had remained with him all his life.

Mishka was undersized. From early spring his hair was the color of sunflower petals. In June the sun scorched it and it went shaggy, unmanageable, and streaked. His cheeks were sprinkled with freckles like a sparrow's egg with speckles. And his nose, from the sun and the constant bathing in the pond kept peeling and was covered with shreds of dry

33

skin. But Mishka had one good feature—his eyes. They looked out through their narrow slits, the lightest blue and roguish, and glistened like chips of river ice.

And it was because of these eyes and his boyish inability to be still that his father was so fond of him. From military service he had brought his son a present of a very stale gingerbread cake and a pair of slightly worn boots. The boots Mishka's mother at once wrapped up in a towel and stored away in the family chest, and the gingerbread cake Mishka consumed that very day to the last crumb after having crushed it with a small hammer.

Next day Mishka woke with the sun. He scooped up a handful of warm water from the pot on the stove, smeared with it yesterday's dirt on his face, and went outside to get dry.

His mother was busy with the cow. His grandfather was sitting on the earthen ledge outside the hut. He called over his grandson and said:

"Crawl under the granary, squirt. A hen was clucking away down there a while ago. She's probably laid an egg. Go get it."

Mishka was always ready to do his grandfather's bidding! He dived on all fours under the granary, crawled out at the other end, and made for the pond, looking back to see whether his grandfather was watching. As he ran toward the fence he shook the nettles off his legs. In the meantime his grandfather sat there waiting, grunting softly, as old men do. At last he got tired of waiting and himself crawled under the granary. He screwed up his eyes to shield them from the steaming heat, knocked his head painfully against the crossbeams but kept on and reached the other end.

"You're a little idiot, Mishka, I swear. Where did you crawl to? No hen would lay her egg here—look near that stone, that's where you'll find it. Where the devil are you, you wicked little rascal?"

Silence. Brushing off his clothes, the old man gazed to-

34

ward the pond, saw his grandson, and shook his fist in his direction.

The kids at the pond surrounded Mishka and started in:

"Was your daddy away in the war?"

"Yes, he was."

"What did he do there?"

"You know what—he fought!"

"That's a lie. All he killed there was bugs, and he went begging for food."

The boys roared with laughter, taunting Mishka, and poking him with their fingers. The bitter insult brought tears to his eyes, and to make matters worse, Vitka, the priest's son, punched him.

"Isn't your father a Communist?" he asked.

"I don't know . . ."

"I know—he is a Communist. This morning my daddy said he's sold his soul to the devil. And he also said all Communists will soon be strung up."

The other boys said nothing, but Mishka's heart sank. They'd hang his daddy, but what for? He gritted his teeth and cried:

"My dad's got a big huge gun and he'll get them, all those bloodsuckers."

Vitka put one foot forward and said triumphantly:

"Your father has short arms. My daddy won't give him a holy blessing and without that he can do nothing."

Proshka, the storekeeper's son, blowing up his nostrils, poked Mishka in the chest and shouted:

"You stop boasting about your father. He took things from my father when the Revolution began and my father said: 'When this government falls, I'll kill Foma the herdsman first of all.'"

Natasha, Proshka's sister, cried shaking her fist:

"Let him have it, boys, why do you stand there doing nothing."

"Beat him up, the Communist's son."

"Kick him hard, Proshka."

Proshka swung a stick and struck Mishka on the shoulder. Vitka stuck out his foot and Mishka went flying headlong, hitting the ground with a thud.

The boys roared and threw themselves on him. Natasha shrieked and scratched Mishka's neck with her nails. Someone kicked him hard in the stomach.

Shaking Proshka off, Mishka jumped up, then getting down on all fours, wriggled off like a chased hare, and dashed home. They whistled after him, threw a stone, but they didn't pursue him.

Mishka caught his breath only when he plunged into the green prickly hemp bushes. He squatted on the damp, fragrant earth, wiped the blood from his scratches and burst into tears. Overhead, pushing its rays through the greenery, the sun tried to look into Mishka's eyes, dried his tears and gently, like his mother, kissed the top of his head.

He sat there for a long time, until his eyes were all dry, then he rose and slowly wandered into his yard.

His father was at the shed, smearing the wheels of the wagon with grease. His army cap had moved way to the back of his head, and he was wearing a blue jersey with white stripes across his chest. Mishka approached him sideways and stood near the wagon. For a long time he said nothing. At last, getting bolder, he nudged his father and asked in a whisper:

"Daddy, what did you do in the war?"

His father smiled into his red whiskers, and said:

"I fought, sonny."

"But the boys . . . the boys say you killed bugs there."

The tears rose again in Mishka's throat. His father laughed and picked him up in his arms.

"They're telling lies, my son. I sailed on a ship. This big ship sailed on the sea, and I was on it. And then I went off to fight."

"Who did you fight with?"

"I fought the gentry, my dear. You're still small, so I had to go to war in your place. There is a song we daddies sing about that."

His father smiled, and tapping the time with his foot, began to sing softly:

Oh, Mishka, Mishka, my dear lad,
Don't go to war, let your dad go instead.
He's seen much of the world, he's old and strong,
You're not even married, you're still so young.

Mishka forgot the insults from the boys. He laughed as he looked at his father's whiskers which stuck out like a bunch of twigs that his mother tied to a stick to make a broom, while below the whiskers his lips smacked noisily and his open mouth formed a round hole as he sang the high notes.

"Now, son, run along," his father said, putting him down. "I must finish fixing this wagon. When you go to bed this evening, I'll tell you all about the war."

The day dragged on like an endless empty road across the steppe. The sun set, the herd came home through the village, the dust settled after they had passed, and the first pale star peeked down shyly from the darkening sky.

Mishka was dying of impatience, but his mother seemed almost on purpose to spend too long a time fussing with the cow, straining the milk, and when she went down into the cellar, she stayed there what seemed like a whole hour. Mishka clung to her like a burr.

"Are we going to eat soon?"

"It's not time yet, you fidget. Always starving!"

But Mishka was determined. He wouldn't move one step from her side. If she went down to the cellar, he'd go after her, when she returned to the kitchen, he'd follow her, nagging: "Mommie, let's eat."

"Now get away from me, you pest! If you're that hungry, get a piece of bread and stuff yourself."

Still, Mishka didn't give up. Even a slap from his mother made no difference. At suppertime he managed somehow to gulp down the hot soup. He dashed into the best room, flung his pants behind the family chest, dived at a run into bed under his mother's patchwork quilt, and lay there peacefully, waiting for his father to come and tell him all about the war.

His grandfather was kneeling before the icon, whispering a prayer and bowing his head all the way to the floor. Mishka looked up and saw the old man bending over with difficulty, supporting himself with the fingers of his left hand pressed against the floor. Beating his forehead against the board, he went—*bang*. And Mishka knocked his elbow against the wall—*bang*.

His grandfather kept whispering and banging his head in obeisance. Mishka kept banging his elbow against the wall in unison. The old man grew angry and turned to the boy.

"I'll show you, you cursed child, Lord forgive me! You knock after me and I'll knock you one."

There would have been a skirmish, but Mishka's father came into the room just in time.

"Why are you in this bed, Mishka?" he asked.

"I sleep with Mommie."

His father sat down on the bed and silently began to twist his mustache. After a moment's thought he said:

"No, I've made up your bed with Grandpa."

"I won't sleep with him."

"Why not?"

"His beard stinks too much of tobacco."

His father twisted his whiskers again and said:

"No, sonny, you go and sleep with Grandpa."

"All right, you can sleep here." Mishka said with a sigh of resignation. "But you will tell me about the war, won't you?"

"I will."

40

The grandfather took the side at the wall and Mishka lay down at the edge. A little later his father came in. He moved a bench over to the bed, sat down, and lit a strong cigarette.

"You see, it was like this. You remember how the store-keeper used to plant his grain right up at our barn?"

Mishka remembered the way he used to run through the tall fragrant wheat. He would climb over the stone wall at the barn and dive into the grain. It covered him right over his head, the heavy, black-whiskered ears tickling his face. The grain smelled of dust, camomile, and the wind from the steppe. His mother used to say to him:

"Don't go far into the field, Minuyshka, you'll get lost."

His father was silent for a moment, then said, stroking his son on the head:

"And do you remember when you and I drove out to Sandy Hill one day? We used to have a piece of land out there . . ."

And Mishka again remembered that along the roadside a little way beyond Sandy Hill there had been a narrow wind-ing strip of grain. One day Mishka went there with his father and they found the strip had been trodden down and ruined by cattle. The grain lay in dirty bunches stamped right into the ground, the empty stalks swaying in the wind. Mishka re-membered how his father, big and strong as he was, had looked stricken and tears ran down his dusty cheeks. Mishka had cried too as he looked at him.

On the way back, his father had asked the watchman minding the vegetable plots:

"Can you tell me, Fiodot, who ruined my field?"

The watchman had spat down at his feet and replied:

"The storekeeper took some cattle to the market place and drove them through your strip on purpose."

Now his father moved the bench still closer to the bed, and began to talk:

"The storekeeper and others of his kind owned most of the land and the poor people had nowhere to sow. And it was

41

like that all over our country, not only in this village. They made it very tough for us in those days. It was hard to keep from starving. I hired myself out as a herdsman, and soon I was sent off to do military service. Men had a hard time in the Army, too; the officers punched you in the face for the least thing. But then the Bolsheviks showed up, and their head is called Lenin. To look at him, you wouldn't think he was so special, but he had a very wise mind, although he came of peasant stock. The Bolsheviks talked such good sense to us that we just stood there with our mouths open. 'What are you standing there catching flies for, workers and peasants?' they said to us. 'Get rid of the masters and the officials in one shake of a lamb's tail, and take what's coming to you.'

"And with those words they really started something. We began to use our heads and decided that what they said was true. We took the land and properties from those who had too much and gave it to those who had nothing or almost nothing. But the masters didn't want to give up their former ways, they were furious and made war on the workers and peasants. Do you understand what I'm saying, sonny?

"And that same Lenin, the elder of the Bolsheviks, stirred up the poor people just like a plowman turns over the ground with his plow. He gathered the soldiers and workers and went after the masters until the down and feathers began to fly off them. These soldiers and workers got to be known as the Red Guard. And I served in this Red Guard. We stayed in a very large house in a very large city. It was called Smolny. The halls in this house are so long, sonny, and it has so many rooms that you could get lost in it very easily.

"I was standing guard at the entrance to this house one night. It was cold outside, and I had only my overcoat on. The wind pierced right through you, right to the bone. Two men came out of this house and walked toward me. They came close and I recognized one of them—it was Lenin. He came over to me and asked kindly:

42

"'Aren't you cold, comrade?'

"But I answer: 'No, comrade Lenin, neither the cold nor the enemy will lick us. We didn't take power into our hands to give it back to the lords and masters.'

"He laughed and shook my hand hard, and then walked quietly to the gate."

Mishka's father was silent for a while, then he reached in his pocket for his tobacco pouch, rolled himself a cigarette, and struck a match, and on his finger Mishka noticed a bright and shining little tear, just like a drop of dew at the end of a nettle.

"That's the kind of man he was. He thought of everybody. He felt sorry for every soldier. After that evening I saw him often. He'd come walking past me, and would recognize me when he was still quite a long way off. Then he'd smile and ask me:

"'So, nothing will lick us, you say?'

"'No one is clever enough for that, comrade Lenin,' I would reply.

"And, do you know, sonny, it all happened just as he said. We took over the land and the factories and got rid of the bloodsuckers. When you grow big, never forget that your daddy was once a soldier and that for four years he shed his blood for the commune, for justice. I'll be dead by then, and Lenin too, but our deeds will live on through the ages. When you grow up you'll fight for the Soviet government like your old man did. Will you?"

"I will!" Mishka cried, and jumped up on the bed, meaning to throw himself on his father's neck. But he forgot his grandfather lying there near him and stepped on his stomach.

The grandfather groaned fiercely and stretched out his hand to grab Mishka by the hair. But Mishka's father picked him up in his arms and carried him into the best room.

And in his arms Mishka fell asleep. Before dropping off he thought a long time about that strange man named

Lenin, about the Bolsheviks, and the fighting. For a while he heard a low hum of conversation through his drowsiness, and he was aware of a pleasant smell of sweat and tobacco, then his eyelids stuck together as though someone gently pressed them down with his hands.

He dreamed about the city almost as soon as he fell asleep: wide streets, chickens bathing in the strewn ashes—there were always plenty of chickens in the village, but there, in the city, there were many, many more. The buildings were exactly the way his father described them: a big huge hut, covered with fresh straw, and on its chimney stood another hut, and on that one's chimney still another, and the chimney of the one at the very top stuck right into the sky.

As Mishka walked along the street, craning his head, trying to see everything, a man in a red shirt appeared from nowhere and walked toward him.

"See here, Mishka, why are you hanging around doing nothing?" he asked kindly.

"My grandpa told me to go out and play," Mishka replied.

"Do you know who I am?"

"No, I don't."

"I'm comrade Lenin."

Mishka's knees shook with fright. He wanted to flee but the man in the red shirt took him by the sleeve and said:

"You haven't enough conscience worth a broken penny, Mishka. You know very well I'm fighting for the poor, then why don't you join my army?"

"My grandpa won't let me," Mishka tried to excuse himself.

"You do as you wish," comrade Lenin said, "but I can't get along without you. You've got to join my army, that's all there is to it."

Mishka then took him by the hand and said very firmly:

"All right, then, I'll join your army without his permission and I'll fight for the poor people. But if Grandpa tries to give me a beating with a switch because I disobeyed him, you must protect me."

"Of course I'll protect you," Lenin said, and walked away down the street. Mishka was breathless with joy! He couldn't breathe, tried to cry out, but his tongue stuck. He shuddered violently, kicked his grandfather with both feet, and woke up.

His grandfather groaned and chewed his lips in his sleep. Through the little window the sky beyond the pond was turning softly pale, and the clouds piling up from the east were edged with rose-colored foam.

III

After that Mishka's father told him about the war every evening, and about Lenin, and the countries he had seen.

One Saturday evening the watchman of the Executive Committee building brought over a short, stocky man in a long coat and carrying a leather brief case. He called Mishka's grandfather and said:

"I've brought a Soviet worker to stay with you, Grandfather. He's from the town and we'd like you to put him up for the night and give him some supper."

"Oh, of course, we don't mind," Grandpa said. "But have you the order, Mister Comrade?"

Mishka was impressed with his grandfather's learning, and sticking a finger in his mouth, hung around to hear what it was all about.

"I have, Daddy, I've got everything," the man with the leather brief case smiled, and he went into the best room.

Grandfather followed him, and Mishka followed his grandfather.

"And what affairs have brought you to us?" the old man asked as they went in.

"I've come to hold new elections. We're going to elect a chairman and members of the Soviet."

A little later Mishka's father came in from the barn. He

greeted the stranger and asked his wife to get some supper ready. After the meal his father and the stranger sat side by side on the bench. The stranger unfastened his brief case, took out a bundle of papers and began showing them to the father. Mishka couldn't control his curiosity and hung around trying to get a peep at them. His father picked up one of the papers and showed it to him, saying:

"Look, Mishka, this is Lenin."

Mishka tore the small card from his father's hand, fixed his gaze on it and opened his mouth in astonishment. On the card was a full-length image of a man not tall and not even wearing a red shirt, but a jacket. One hand was in his trouser pocket, the other was pointing to something in the distance. Mishka looked at him closely and took the whole picture in at a single glance—the knitted brows, the smile hovering on his pleasant face and in the corners of the mouth. He memorized every detail of the features.

The stranger took the picture from Mishka, snapped the lock of the brief case, and went off to bed. He undressed, lay down, and covered himself with his coat. He was dozing off when he heard the door creak. He raised his head.

"Who's there?"

He heard someone's bare feet on the floor.

"Who's there?" he asked again, then saw Mishka standing near his bed.

"What do you want, youngster?"

Mishka stood for a while without speaking, then gathering up courage, said in a whisper:

"Uncle, I'll tell you what—how about giving me Lenin."

The stranger did not answer and just stared at the boy.

Mishka became uneasy—suppose the man was a miser and wouldn't give him the picture? Trying to control the quiver in his voice, hurrying and swallowing some of the words, he whispered:

"You give it to me for keeps, and I'll give you a tin box, a good one, and I'll give you all my knucklebones," and waving his hand in resignation, he added: "And I'll give you the boots my daddy brought me from the service."

"And what are you going to do with Lenin?" the stranger asked with a smile.

"He won't let me have him," Mishka decided. He hung his head low so that the man wouldn't see his tears, and said thickly:

"I just need it."

The stranger laughed, took his brief case from under the pillow and handed Mishka the card. Mishka slipped it under his shirt, hugged it tightly, and trotted out of the best room. His grandfather woke up and scolded:

"Why are you wandering around, you owl?"

Mishka lay down without saying a word. He lay on his back holding the card in both hands. He was afraid to turn over in case he creased it and he slept that way the rest of the night.

He woke up before dawn. His mother had milked the cow and driven it out to join the herd. She saw Mishka, and clapping her hands in surprise, said:

"Now what's possessed you? Why are you up so early?"

He pressed the picture to him, hurried past his mother to the barn and dived under the granary.

Burdocks grew around the granary walls and the nettles rose in a thick green wall. He crawled underneath the granary, chose the spot, brushed aside the dust with his hand, tore off a burdock leaf yellow with age, wrapped the picture in it, and put a small stone on top so that the wind wouldn't blow it away.

It rained all day. The sky was covered with a gray canopy, puddles steamed in the yard, and little streams chased each other down the street.

Mishka had to stay in the house all day. Toward evening his father and grandfather went off to the meeting in the Executive Committee building. Mishka put on his grandfather's peaked cap and ran after them. Breathless, he climbed up the creaking, mud-covered steps to the porch and went into the room. Tobacco smoke floated under the ceiling, the place was jammed with people. The stranger was sitting at a table by the window, talking with some of the assembled Cossacks.

Mishka slipped quietly into a seat at the back.

Prokhor Lisenkov, the storekeeper's son-in-law, sitting just in front of Mishka, shouted:

"Citizens, I propose you take him off the list of candidates. His conduct has been indecent. We saw that plainly even when he was a herdsman."

Mishka saw Fiodor the shoemaker rise from his seat on the window sill and shout, waving his arms with excitement:

"Comrades, the rich don't want a poor herdsman to be chairman. But because he's a worker and on the side of the Soviet government . . ."

Standing in a bunch by the door, the well-to-do Cossacks stamped their feet, whistled, and shouted in unison:

"We don't want the herdsman."

"Now that he's through with his military service, let him become a herdsman again."

"To hell with Foma Korshunov."

Mishka glanced at the pale face of his father, who was standing near a bench and he, too, went white with fear for him.

"Less noise, comrades. I'll have you put out if you don't quiet down," the stranger yelled, banging his fist on the table.

"We'll elect one of our men, a Cossack."

We don't want him! We don't want him!"

"We say, blast him," the Cossacks howled, and Prokhor, the storekeeper's son-in-law louder than the rest.

A husky, red-bearded Cossack in a ragged, patched jacket, and with an earring in one ear, jumped on to a bench.

"Brothers! You can see what's happening. The rich want to put their own man in as chairman. And then again to . . ."

Through the uproar Mishka understood only some of the words the Cossack with the earring was shouting:

"When the land's . . . allotted . . . the poor will get the clay . . . they'll take the black earth for themselves."

"Prokhor for chairman," the bunch near the door yelled.

"Pro . . . khor . . . Ho-ho-ho! Ha-ha-ha!"

The stranger coped energetically with the hubbub, knitting his brows and shouting again and again:

"I suppose he's cursing," Mishka thought.

At last the stranger asked in a hoarse voice:

"Who's for Foma Korshunov?"

Many hands went up. Mishka raised his hand too. Someone jumped from bench to bench counting out loud.

"Sixty-three, sixty-four . . ." and without noticing Mishka himself, the man pointed to the boy's raised hand and cried: "Sixty-five."

"Those in favor of Prokhor Lisenkov, please raise their hands."

Twenty-seven rich Cossacks and Yegor, the miller, put up their hands. Mishka looked about him and put up his hand again. The man counting the votes looked him up and down and seized him painfully by the ear.

"You ragamuffin! Clear out or I'll throw you out. You voting too!"

A laugh arose from the crowd, but the man led Mishka to the door and pushed him in the back. Mishka remembered what his father had said when arguing with Grandfather, and as he slipped down the muddy steps, shouted back:

"You have no right!"

"I'll show you my right."

When he got home Mishka cried a little and complained to his mother, but she only said angrily:

"Well, don't go where you aren't wanted. Stop sticking your nose in every hole."

49

IV

Next morning, as they all sat at breakfast, they heard muffled music in the distance. Mishka's father put down his spoon and said, wiping his mustache:

"That's a military band."

Mishka flew off his seat as though blown off by the wind. The porch door slammed and Mishka's rapid steps sounded outside the window.

His father and grandfather followed him into the yard, and his mother leaned out of the window.

At the end of the street ranks of Red Army men were pouring into the village in a green, heaving wave. At their head, musicians were blowing into huge trumpets and the sounds echoed over the entire village.

Mishka's eyes nearly popped out. He danced up and down then tore off and ran up to the band. He had a sweetly tight feeling in his chest, and it rose to his throat. He looked at the dusty faces of the Red Army men and at the musicians puffing out their cheeks importantly, and decided irrevocably, right there and then; "I'll go and fight with them."

He remembered his dream with Lenin and, gaining courage who knows from where, he caught at the knapsack of a man on the outside file, and asked:

"Where are you going? To fight?"

"What else? Of course, to fight."

"On whose side?"

"For the Soviet government, little dunce. Here, get into the middle."

He pushed Mishka into the middle of the rank where someone laughed and stroked his bristly hair. Another took a dusty piece of sugar out of his pocket as he marched along and popped it into the boy's mouth. When they reached the square a voice shouted from in front:

"Ha-a-a-lt!"

The Red Army men came to a halt, scattered over the square, and most of them lay down in small groups in the cool shadow of the school fence. A tall, clean-shaven Red Army man with a sword at his side came up to Mishka and asked, smiling:

"And how did you happen to fall in with us? Where are you from?"

"I'm going off with you, to fight."

"Comrade Combat, take him on as your assistant," one of the Red Army men shouted.

There was a general burst of laughter. Mishka blinked hard, but the man with the odd title of Combat, who was the battalion commander, frowned and shouted sternly:

"What are you laughing at, you idiots? Of course we'll take him with us, but on one condition," and the Combat turned to Mishka and said: "You have only one suspender to your trousers. You can't go around like that, you'd disgrace us. Look, I've got two suspenders and all the other men have two also. Hurry home and get your mother to sew on another suspender for you and we'll wait here until you return." He then turned to the men and shouted, winking: "Tereshchenko, go and fetch for the new recruit an overcoat and a gun."

One of the men resting by the fence rose, put his hand to his cap, answered: "Very good!" and went off quickly.

"Now, on the double! Get your mother to sew on that second suspender."

Mishka gave the Combat a meaningfully stern look, and said:

"You better watch out, don't try any of your tricks on me!"

"What makes you think I'd do a thing like that? Why should I?"

It was some distance from the square to his hut. By the time Mishka reached the gate he was out of breath. He drew off his trousers as he ran through the gate, and, his

51

bare legs gleaming in the sunlight, he burst into the hut.

"Mommie, my pants—sew on another suspender."

Not a sound could be heard inside. A black swarm of flies was buzzing around the stove. Mishka ran into the yard, to the barn, and into the orchard, but couldn't find his mother, his father, or his grandfather. He rushed back into the best room where a sack caught his eye. He hurriedly cut off a long piece with a knife and not knowing how to sew or having time to do it, he tied the strip of sackcloth to his pants, threw it over his shoulder, tied it again in front and rushed outside and under the granary.

There he pushed away the stone, took a quick glance at Lenin's hand pointing at him, and whispered catching his breath:

"You see, I am joining your army right now."

He wrapped the picture with care in the burdock leaf, slipped it inside his shirt, over his heart, and galloped out into the street. He held the picture tightly against him with one hand and supported his pants with the other. When he passed their neighbor's fence he shouted:

"Anisimovna!"

"What do you want?"

"Tell my folks to go ahead and eat dinner without me."

"Where are you off to, you little nut?"

He ignored her remark with a wave of the hand.

"I'm going to join the military service."

He ran all the way to the square and when he reached it, he stopped short as though nailed to the ground. Not a soul was to be seen. Cigarette butts were scattered under the fence, together with empty tin cans and someone's torn puttees. He could hear a muffled rumble of music from the far end of the village and the thud of the marching soldiers' feet against the hard pavement.

A sob burst from Mishka's throat, he cried out and ran with all his small might to catch up with them. And he would have certainly caught up with them had it not been for the yellow, long-tailed dog lying right across the road, baring his teeth at Mishka. By the time he ran around through another street and came back to the main road, he could hear neither the music nor the tramp of the soldiers' feet.

V

A couple of days later a detachment of about forty men came into the village. The soldiers were wearing gray felt boots and soiled workmen's jackets. Mishka's father came home from the Executive Committee building for dinner and told Grandfather:

"You'll have to get the grain in the granary ready, Grandpa. A produce-collecting detachment has arrived. They are making a search for grain. The fighting men have to be fed."

The soldiers went from yard to yard, probed the ground in the barns with their bayonets to find the hidden grain and carted it off to the communal granary.

A few of them called on the new chairman. Their leader, chewing on his pipe, asked Grandfather:

"Have you buried your grain, old man? Come on, admit it."

Grandfather said proudly, stroking his beard:

"Don't you know that my son is one of you?"

In the granary the soldier with the pipe surveyed the bins and smiled.

"Bring out the grain from this corn bin, Grandpa, and you can keep the rest for food and for seed."

The old man harnessed the old horse Savraska to the wagon, grunted and groaned with misery as he filled eight sacks, and carted them to the communal granary. Mishka's mother had cried for a while at the loss of the grain, but he, Mishka, had helped his grandfather pour it into the sacks and then had gone off to play with Vitka, the priest's son.

They had just settled down on the kitchen floor and

53

spread out their horses cut from paper when the same soldiers came in. The priest ran out to meet them, made a fuss over them, and invited them into his house. The soldier with the pipe said sternly:

"Let's go to the granary. Where do you keep your grain?"

The priest's wife came running out of the best room and, smiling slyly, said:

"Believe us, gentlemen, we haven't any grain at all right now. My husband hasn't made the rounds yet for his tithes."

"Do you have a cellar in the house?"

"No, we don't. When we have grain we keep it in the granary."

Mishka remembered that Vitka and he had crawled down into a large cellar once—it was right under the kitchen—and he turned to the priest's wife and said:

"Don't you remember? Vitka and I once climbed down into your cellar from here, from the kitchen."

The woman turned pale, but laughed loudly:

"You're all wrong, youngster. Vitka, why don't you both go out into the yard to play."

The soldier with the pipe narrowed his eyes and smiled at Mishka.

"Show me how you get down there, sonny."

The priest's wife cracked her finger joints nervously and said:

"Don't pay any attention to what this stupid little boy is saying. I assure you, gentlemen, we have no cellar."

And the priest added:

"Could we offer you a bite to eat, comrades? Let's go into the guest room."

When the priest's wife went past Mishka she pinched him hard and smiled gently:

"Go on, go into the garden, children—you're in the way here."

The soldiers winked at one another and went into the kitchen. Pounding the floor with their rifle butts, they moved the table standing at the wall, pulled away a piece of rough sacking covering the floor under it, and lifted a floorboard. They looked down into the cellar, and the soldier with the pipe shook his head.

"Aren't you ashamed of yourselves? You said you had no grain and your cellar is filled to the top with wheat."

The priest's wife gave Mishka such a withering look that he took fright and decided that he had better get back home as quickly as his feet could carry him. He got up and made for the yard. Wailing, she rushed after him, grabbed him by the hair and shook him hard.

He wrenched himself away by force and ran home without looking back. Choking with tears, he complained to his mother about what happened, but she only held her head in dismay.

"What am I going to do with you? Get out of my sight before I give you one, too."

After that, when Mishka was insulted or hurt he would crawl under the granary, move away the stone, unfold the burdock leaf and, wetting Lenin's picture with his tears, would tell him all about his troubles and the people who had mistreated him.

A week passed. Mishka began to be bored. After the incident at the priest's house, he had no one to play with. None of the children would now have anything to do with him. To the nickname of shame-child, they now added another, which they had heard from the grown-ups. They taunted him with:

"Hey, you communist mongrel! You communist brat. You better watch out!"

VI

One day Mishka came home from a lonesome swim late in the afternoon. As he entered the hut he could hear his father talking in sharp tones and his mother crying and lamenting, as if someone had just died. Mishka slipped quietly into the room and saw his father rolling up his heavy coat and then pulling on his boots.

"Are you going away, Daddy?"

His father laughed and answered:

"Here, sonny, console your mother. She's breaking my heart with her sobbing. I'm going off to the war, but she doesn't want me to leave."

"I'm going with you, Daddy."

His father tightened his belt and put on his army cap.

"You're a strange one, I must say. How can both of us go off at the same time? When I come back, then you can go. Otherwise, when the grain ripens, who'll harvest it? Your mother has enough to do around the house, and your grandfather is old."

Mishka held back his tears when he said good-bye to his father. He even managed to smile. But Mishka's mother hung around his neck as on the day of his homecoming. His father had to force her to let him go. The grandfather only moaned and he whispered into his son's ear as he kissed him:

"Foma, my son, maybe you can stay after all. Couldn't they manage without you? You may be killed, and then what will happen to us? We'll all perish."

"Stop that kind of talk, Father. Who's going to defend our new power if every man crawls under his woman's petticoat for protection?

"Oh, go ahead, then, if your cause is just."

The old man turned away and stealthily wiped his tears. They all saw the soldier off as far as the Executive Committee building. Some twenty men with rifles were assembled in the yard. Mishka's father also picked up a rifle and, giving him one last kiss, marched off with the others to the outskirts of the village.

Mishka returned with his grandfather. His mother dragged herself behind them. They could hear a dog's occasional howling and saw a light shining from a window here and there. The village was wrapped in darkness, like an old woman in her black shawl. A fine rain began to fall, and somewhere over the steppe lightning flickered and peals of thunder rolled in the sky.

Mishka was silent most of the way, but when they drew near the house, he asked his grandfather:

"Grandpa, whom is Daddy going to fight?"

"Stop pestering me!"

"Grandpa!"

"Well?"

"Whom is Daddy going to fight?"

The old man answered, as he crossly bolted the gate:

"Evil men have turned up not far from our village. Some call them a band, but I say they're nothing but bandits. Your dad has gone off to fight them."

"Are there many of them, Grandpa?"

"They say there are about two hundred. Now, off to bed with you, little rascal. You've been hanging around long enough."

During that night Mishka was awakened by the sound of voices. He felt for his grandfather in the bed but didn't find him.

"Grandpa, where are you?"

He heard his grandfather answer from the kitchen: "Be quiet and go to sleep, you fidget."

Mishka got out of bed and groped his way in the darkness. His grandfather was sitting on the bench, in his underpants, looking out the open window. He was listening. Mishka heard shots rattling beyond the village in the night's silence, then the steady crash of volley after volley, sounding as though someone were pounding nails into wood.

Mishka was filled with terror. He pressed against his grandfather and began to whimper:

"Is that Daddy shooting?"

His grandfather didn't answer him, but his mother started again to cry and lament.

The firing went on till dawn, then stopped. Mishka curled himself up on the bench like a little twisted loaf and dropped off into a restless sleep. At daybreak a group of horsemen galloped along the street in the direction of the Executive Committee building. His grandfather roused him and they went into the yard.

Smoke soon rose in a black column from the Executive Committee building, and the fire lapped at the surrounding huts. Then more horsemen roamed along the street. One of them cantered up to the yard and yelled to Grandfather:

"Have you got a horse, old man?"

"Yes."

"Then harness it up and go outside the village. Your Communists are lying there in the scrub. Pile them into your wagon and bring them in. Let their families bury them."

Grandfather quickly harnessed up Savraska to the wagon and rode off at a trot.

There was an uproar of shouts in the village. Some of the bandits had dismounted and were dragging hay from the barns and slaughtering sheep. One of them sprang off his horse outside Anisimovna's yard and ran into her hut. Mishka heard her screaming at the top of her voice. Then the bandit ran out to her porch, his saber rattling, sat down, pulled off his boots, tore Anisimovna's flowered best shawl in half, tore off his dirty puttees and wrapped each leg in half the shawl.

Mishka went into the best room, lay down on the bed, and buried his head in the pillow. He stayed there until he heard the gate creak. He ran out on the porch and saw his grandfather leading the horse into the yard. His beard was wet with tears.

A barefoot man was lying with his arms flung out on the bottom of the wagon. His head bounced up and down on the bare boards.

Mishka went up to the wagon unsteadily and glanced at the man's face. It was cut up with saber slashes so badly that it didn't look like a face.

Mishka did not guess who the man was, but he trembled all over with horror, moved his eyes to the body and, seeing the blue and white stripes of the bloodstained shirt, he crumpled as if someone had hit him behind the knees. Staring wildly at the rigid face, he jumped onto the wagon.

"Daddy, get up, my dear daddy!" He fell off the wagon and tried to run away, but his legs gave way under him, and he crawled on all fours to the porch steps and pushed his head into the sand.

VII

His grandfather's eyes were deeply sunken, his head shook all the time, and his lips moved without making a sound.

He sat stroking Mishka on the head not saying a word for a very long time. Then, looking at his daughter-in-law lying prostrate on the bed, he whispered:

"Little grandson, let's go outside."

He took Mishka by the hand and walked with him to the porch. As they went past the best room, Mishka screwed up his eye and shuddered. On the table in that room his father lay, soundless and solemn. They had washed the blood off him, but Mishka still saw him as he had looked on the wagon.

Grandfather went to the well and fumbled with the rope for a long time, untying the pail. Then he went into the barn, led out Savraska, wiped the bay's frothy lips with his sleeve, and bridled her, listening all the time to the sounds echoing from the village—to the shouts and laughter. Two men rode by, their cigarettes glowing in the darkness, and their voices could be heard clearly:

"They'll never forget the kind of grain requisition we've carried out on them! They'll even remember in the next world how we took their grain."

The sounds of their horses' hoofs died away. Grandfather bent down to Mishka and whispered:

59

"I'm old . . . I can't mount the horse . . . I'll put you on it, little grandson, and you go with God's help to Pronin village . . . I'll show you the way you must go. . . . That Red detachment that came through here with music yesterday ought to be there by now. . . . Tell them to come back to the village—tell them the bandits are here. Did you get that?"

Mishka nodded without speaking. The old man raised him and seated him on the horse, tied his legs with the rope to the saddle so that he wouldn't fall off, then led Savraska through the barn, to the pond, and past the bandit guard into the steppe.

"On the hillock you'll find a gully running up into the hill. Ride straight up, don't turn to the right or left. That path will take you straight to Pronin. Now go, my dear."

The old man kissed him and gave Savraska a gentle smack with his hand.

The night was moonlit and clear. With a snort Savraska started off at a gentle trot, but feeling the light load on her back, she increased her speed. Mishka used the reins for a whip, smacked his horse's neck to make her go faster, and he shook and bounced as she increased her speed.

A quail whistled boldly somewhere in the green thicket of ripening grain. A spring tinkled at the bottom of the gully, the wind blew a cool current of air.

Mishka was scared to find himself alone in the steppe. He put his arms around Savraska's neck and pressed against the warm animal like a little bundle of chilliness.

The gully wound upward, then descended again, and rose once more. Mishka was too frightened to look back. He whispered to himself in an effort not to think of anything. The silence stuck in his ears and he kept his eyes closed.

Savraska tossed her head, snorted, and quickened her pace. After a while Mishka opened his eyes and saw below small pale yellow lights. The wind brought the sound of barking to his ears.

His little heart leaped with joy. He prodded Savraska with his heels and urged her on.

The dog's barking sounded nearer. Cocks began to crow over the sleepy village.

"Halt! Who goes there? Halt or I fire!"

Frightened, Mishka pulled on the reins, but his horse smelled the nearness of other horses, and with a whinny broke into a gallop, ignoring the reins.

"Halt!"

Shots rang out from the windmill. Mishka's cry was drowned in the thud of Savraska's hoofs. She groaned, reared up, and came down heavily on her flank.

Mishka felt a terrible, unbearable stab in his right foot. The shout died on his lips. The horse pressed more and more heavily on his foot.

The sound of approaching horsemen drew closer. Two men galloped up with clattering sabers. They leaped off their horses and bent over Mishka.

"Heavens! it's that same little boy!"

"We haven't killed him!?"

One of them felt Mishka's heart and said with relief:

"He's alive!, but the horse has crushed his foot."

As he was losing consciousness, Mishka whispered:

"The bandits are in our village. They killed my daddy. They burnt down the Executive Committee building. Grandpa told me to ride here as fast as I could."

Circles of light spun before his eyes. He saw his daddy twisting his red mustache and laughing, but there was a gash across his eye. Grandfather walked past shaking his head disapprovingly, then his mother came, then a short, big-browed man with his outstretched hand. His hand pointed straight at Mishka.

"Comrade Lenin!" Mishka cried out in a thin, shaking voice, and he raised his head with difficulty, smiled, and stretched both arms toward him.

1925

The Fate of a Man

I

THERE WAS AN unusual benevolence and drive in the spring
that came to the reaches of the Upper Don in the first year
after the war. At the end of March warm winds began to
blow from the Sea of Azov, and within two days there was
no trace of snow on the river's sandy left bank. In the steppe
the snow-packed valleys and gullies swelled with the thaw
that was bursting the ice, the streams of the steppe flooded
madly, and the roads became almost impassable.

In this season so unfavorable for travel, it happened that
I had to go to the village of Bukanovskaya. The distance
was not great, only about sixty kilometers, but it turned out
not to be so simple a matter. My friend and I started out
before sunrise. Our well-fed horses strained but could hardly
pull the heavy carriage. The wheels sank axle-deep into the
mush of sand, snow, and ice, and in an hour creamy white
drops of foam appeared on their flanks and thighs as well as
under the narrow harness bands, and the fresh morning air
became filled with the sharp, intoxicating smell of horses'
sweat mingled with that of warm tar lavishly smeared over
the trappings.

Where the going was particularly hard for the horses, we
got out of the carriage and walked. It was difficult to walk
in the deep slush squishing under our boots, but the sides
of the road were still coated with a crystal coat of ice glisten-

ing in the sun, and there it was even more difficult to proceed. It took us about six hours to cover the thirty kilometers that brought us to the crossing of the Yelanka River.

The narrow river, parts of which were almost dry in the summer, had now flooded over a full kilometer of marshy meadows overgrown with alders. We had to make the crossing in a leaky flat-bottomed boat which could not hold more than two people at a time. We freed the horses. In a collective farm cart-shed on the other side of the flooded meadows, an old dilapidated jeep that had been standing there most of the winter was awaiting us. The driver and I climbed into the flimsy boat with some misgivings. My friend stayed behind on the bank with our things. We had scarcely pushed off when little fountains of water began to spout up through several chinks in the boat's rotting bottom. We plugged up this hopeless craft with anything at hand and kept bailing until we reached shore. It took us an hour to get to the other side of the Yelanka. The driver brought out the jeep and returned to the boat.

"If this cursed tub doesn't fall apart in the water," he said lifting an oar, "we'll be back in a couple of hours. Don't expect us sooner."

The farm was a good distance from the river, and at the river edge there was the kind of stillness that fills deserted places only in the depths of autumn or at the early beginnings of spring. The air from the river was damp and sharp with the bitter smell of rotting alders, but from the adjacent steppe, now bathed in a lilac haze of mist, a light wind carried the eternally young, faint scent of earth that has recently been freed from the winter's snow.

A broken wattle fence lay on the sand at the water's edge. I sat down on it and was going to have a smoke, but when I put my hand into the inside pocket of my padded jacket, I discovered to my great disappointment that the package of cigarettes I had been carrying in it was soaking wet. During the crossing a wave had washed over the side of the careening boat and had drenched me to the waist with murky water. It had been the wrong moment to think about my cigarettes, for I had to drop my oar and instantly start bailing as fast as I could to save the boat from sinking. But now, annoyed at my own negligence, I pulled the soaked package out of my pocket, got down on my haunches, and began to spread the moist brownish cigarettes on the fence.

It was noon. The sun was hot, as in May. I hoped the cigarettes would soon dry. It was so hot that I began to regret having put on my quilted army trousers and jacket for the trip. It was the first really warm day of the year. But it felt good to sit there alone, abandoning myself completely to the stillness and solitude, and to take off my old army *ushanka,* a fur hat with flaps for the ears, letting the breeze dry my hair that had got wet with the heavy work of rowing. I sat there watching idly the white broadchested clouds piling up in the light blue of the sky.

Presently I saw a man come out into the road from behind the end huts of the farm. He was leading a little boy by the hand, not more than five or six years old, judging by his size. They walked wearily toward the crossing, but on reaching the jeep they turned and came in my direction. The tall and rather stooped man came right up to me and said in a husky, bass voice:

"Hello, neighbor."

"Hello." I shook the big calloused hand he offered me.

The man bent down to the child and said:

"Say hello to the uncle, my boy. Guess he's also a driver, like your old man. But you and I used to drive a truck, didn't we, and he chases about in that little car over there."

Looking straight at me with a pair of eyes as clear as the sky that day, and smiling a little, the boy confidently held out a cold pink hand. I shook it lightly and asked:

"Why's your hand so cold, old man? It's hot today, but you're freezing."

With a touching childish trust the boy leaned against my knees and lifted his little flaxen eyebrows in surprise.

"What makes you think I'm an old man, uncle? I'm a real boy, and I'm really not freezing at all. My hands are cold because I've been throwing snowballs, that's why."

Taking the nearly empty knapsack off his back, the father sat down wearily beside me and said:

"This passenger of mine is a lot of trouble! It's because of him that I'm so tuckered out. You take a long step, he breaks into a trot. Just try to keep up with an infantryman like him. At other times, where I could take only one step, I have to take three instead, and so it goes—we march along out of step, like a horse and a turtle. And I need two pairs of eyes to know what he's up to. As soon as your back is turned he's off wading in a puddle or breaking off an icicle and sucking it instead of a candy. No, it's not a job for a man to be traveling with a passenger like him, at least not on foot." He was silent for a while then asked:

"And what about you, friend? Waiting for your chief?"

I somehow felt hesitant about telling him that I wasn't a driver. I answered:

"Yes, you know how it is, at times there is no helping it, you've got to wait around."

"Is he coming over from across the river?"

"Yes."

"Do you know if the boat will be here soon?"

"In about two hours."

"That's quite a while. Well, a rest will do us good. We've no place to hurry. I saw you as I walked by, so I thought to myself: There's one of us drivers getting a bit of suntan. 'Go ahead,' I said to myself, 'have a smoke with him.' It's lonesome to smoke alone and to die in loneliness. You're living rich, I see, smoking bought cigarettes. Got them wet, eh? Well, brother, wet tobacco is like a patched up horse, neither of them is any good. Let's roll our own instead."

He reached in his pocket and brought out a worn, raspberry-colored silk pouch, and as he unrolled it, I managed to read the embroidered words on the corner: "To one of our dear fighters, from a sixth-grade student of Lebedyanskaya Secondary School."

We smoked the strong home-grown tobacco and both of us were silent for a while. I was going to ask him where he was going with the boy and what had brought him out on such slushy roads, but he beat me to it with his question:

"And you, neighbor, were you in for the duration?"

"Almost."

"At the front?"

"Yes."

"Well, friend, I was drowned in a heap of troubles myself, up to my eyes, and then some."

He rested his large dark hands on his knees and let his shoulders droop. I glanced at him sideways and felt strangely moved. Have you ever seen eyes that look as if they have been sprinkled with ashes, eyes filled with such mortal anguish that it is too painful to look into them? Well, this is the way the eyes of my new acquaintance looked.

He broke a dry twisted twig from the fence and for a minute silently traced some odd pattern in the sand with it. Then he spoke again:

"There are times when I can't sleep at night, I lie there staring empty-eyed into the darkness and think: 'Life, why did you cripple me like this? Why did you keep punishing me?' And I get no answer, neither in the night, nor in bright sunshine. No answer comes, and I'll never get one!" He caught himself suddenly, pushed his little boy affectionately, and said:

"Go on, darling, go and play down by the water, there's always something a little boy can find to do near a big river. Just be sure not to get your feet wet."

While we had been smoking together in silence, I had stealthily taken stock of the father and the son, and I observed one thing that seemed strange to me. The boy was

69

dressed plainly, but his clothes were good. His long jacket, lined with used fur, fitted him well, his tiny boots were large enough to leave room for heavy woolen socks, and the patch on the sleeve of his jacket had been carefully sewn on, showing the skillful hand of a mother. But the father's appearance was quite different. His padded jacket, scorched in several places, had been carelessly and poorly mended, the patch on his threadbare khaki trousers had not been sewn on properly; it was tacked on with large, uneven man's stitches. Although he had on an almost new pair of army boots, the tops of his woolen socks were full of moth holes—they had obviously never known the touch of a woman's hand. I thought: Either he's a widower or there was something not right between him and his wife.

He watched his son running off to play, coughed to clear his throat, and began to speak again, and I was all attention.

"At first my life was ordinary. I come from Voronezh province—was born there, in 1900. During the Civil War I was in the Red Army, in Kikvidze's division. During the famine of 'twenty-two I went to the Kuban district and worked like an ox there for the rich peasants—that's what saved me from starving to death. But my father, mother, and little sister died of hunger. I was the only one of us who survived. As for relatives, I didn't have a single one, not a soul. Well, after a year I came back from the Kuban, sold my little hut, and went to Voronezh. First I worked as a carpenter, then I got work at a factory where I learned to be a locksmith. Soon after that I got married. My wife had been brought up in a children's home. She was an orphan. Yes, I got myself a good woman! Good-natured, cheerful, eager to please me, and smart, too—much smarter than me. She had known from childhood what a peck of trouble cost, you could tell that from her character. Just to look at her, she wasn't that good-looking, but, you see, that's not the way I looked at her. For me there was no woman more beautiful than she, and there never will be!

70

"I'd come from work tired, and, at times, bad-tempered as the devil. But, no, she'd never answer with a nasty word when I used some. Gentle and calm, she couldn't do enough for you, always trying to surprise me with a treat of some kind, even when there wasn't enough food around. It lifted my heart just to look at her. After being mean I'd put my arm around her and say: 'Forgive me, Irina dear, I was rotten mean to you—things were terrible at work today.' And there'd be peace between us once more, and my heart would be at rest. And you know, brother, how important that is for a man's work. Next morning I'd jump out of bed and go off to the factory and any job I'd tackle that day would go like clockwork. That's what it means to have a smart woman and a pal for a wife.

"Once in a while I'd get drunk with the boys on pay-day. And once in a while, the way I staggered home afterward must have been pretty disgusting. Even the main street wasn't wide enough for me then, let alone the side streets. In those days I was healthy and husky as the devil, and I could hold a lot of liquor—I'd always get home on my own. But there were times when I'd make the last stretch in lowest gear, I'd finish by crawling on all fours. Even then there was no fuss, no screaming, no scene from Irina. She'd just giggle, my Irina, and she'd do even that with caution, so that I'd not take it wrong in my drunken state. She'd pull my boots off and whisper: 'Lie down near the wall, Andriusha, or you'll fall off the bed in your sleep.' And I'd flop down like a sack of oats and everything would swim before my eyes. But I'd feel her stroking my head gently as I dropped off to sleep, and I'd know she was feeling sorry for me.

"In the morning she'd get me up about two hours earlier than usual to give me time to pull myself together for work. She knew I couldn't eat anything because of the hangover, so she'd get me a pickle or something light like that and pour me a glass of vodka. 'Here, this will help you sober up,

71

Andriusha, but don't do this again, my dear!' Tell me, how could any man violate such trust in him? I'd take that drink, thank her without words, just with a look, kiss her, and go off to work like a lamb. But if she had had a cross word for me when drunk, if she had yelled or sworn at me, God is my witness, I'd have got drunk the very next day. That's the way things go in other families, that is, where the wife is a fool. I've seen enough of them, and I know what I'm talking about.

"So, soon the children started coming. First my little son was born, Anatoly, then two girls. And that was when I quit drinking. I began to bring all my wages home to the wife. We had a fair-sized family by then and it made no sense to keep on with the drinking. On my day off I'd have just a glass of beer and let it go at that.

"In 'twenty-nine I began to be interested in cars. I studied about engines, learned to drive, and got work as a trucker. When I had got the hang of it, I didn't feel like going on at the factory. Behind the wheel a day's work was more fun. And this is the way ten years flew by. I hardly noticed them. They passed as in a dream. But what's ten years? Ask any grown man if he'd noticed how the years have slipped by. He hadn't noticed a damn thing! The past is like that steppe in the distance, out there in the haze. As I was walking across it this morning it was clear all around me, but now that I've covered twenty kilometers there's a haze over the distance I've walked, and you can't tell the trees from the steppe grass, the grainfield from the hayfield.

"I worked day and night during those ten years. I earned good money and we lived no worse than other folk. And the children brought us joy: all three of them got excellent grades in school, and the oldest, my Anatoly, was so bright in mathematics that he even got his name into a big newspaper. Where he got such a talent for science, I couldn't tell you. But it sure pleased me a lot, I was proud of him, and how!

"In those ten years we saved up a bit of money, and before the war we built ourselves a small house with two rooms, a pantry, and a little porch. Irina bought herself a couple of goats. What more did we need? There was milk for the children's *kasha,* we had a roof over our heads, clothes on our backs, shoes on our feet, so everything was all right. Only, it was our poor luck to have chosen the wrong spot to build on. The plot of land we got was just six hundred feet from an aircraft factory. If my little shanty had been somewhere else, maybe my life would have turned out different.

"And then, there it was—the war! I was called up the very next day, and the day after that it was 'please report to your troop train.' My four saw me off: Irina, Anatoly, and my two daughters, Nastenka and Olyushka. The children behaved well—they had themselves under control. Of course, there were tears in the girls' eyes. Anatoly's shoulders twitched a bit, as if with cold—he was going on seventeen by that time. But that Irina of mine—I'd never seen her carry on that way, not in all the seventeen years we had been together. All night my shoulder and shirt didn't get a chance to dry from her tears, and in the morning there were more tears. We got to the station. I felt so sorry for her, I could hardly look at her. Her lips were swollen from crying, her hair was loose under her kerchief, and her eyes were dull and without any expression, as if she was out of her mind. When the officers gave the order to get aboard, she flung herself on me, locked her hands around my neck, and was shaking all over, like a tree that's been struck down. The children tried to calm her and I did too, but nothing helped. Other women stood there just talking to their husbands or sons, but mine clung to me like a leaf to a branch, trembling all the time, and she couldn't say a word. 'Get a grip on yourself, Irina, my darling,' I said, 'say something to me before I go, at least one word.' And this is what she said, with a sob between every word: 'My very own . . . Andriusha

. . . we'll never . . . see each other again . . . in this world. . . .'

"There am I, my heart broken in pieces with pity for her, and she goes and says a thing like that to me! She ought to have understood it wasn't easy for me either to part with them. After all, I wasn't going off to a pancake party. So my evil temper got the better of me. I forced her hands apart, freed myself, and gave her a slight push in the shoulder. It seemed only a gentle push to me, but I was a strong fool and she staggered back about three paces, then came toward me again with little helpless steps, her arms stretched out, and I shouted at her: 'Is that the way to say good-bye? Why are you burying me while I'm still alive!?' Well, I took her in my arms again because I could see she was not herself."

He broke off in the middle, and in the silence that followed I heard a choking sound coming from his throat. His grief communicated itself to me. I glanced sideways at him but did not see a single tear in those lifeless eyes of his. He sat with his head lowered dismally. His large hands hung limp at his sides. They were shaking slightly. His chin trembled, and so did his firm lips.

II

"Don't, my friend, don't think about it," I said softly. He probably didn't even hear me. Conquering his emotion with a great effort, he said abruptly, in a hoarse, strangely different voice:

"Till my dying day, till the last hour of my life, I'll never forgive myself for having pushed her away like that!"

He was silent again, and for a long time. He tried to roll a cigarette, but the piece of paper tore in his fingers and the tobacco scattered over his knees. In the end he managed somehow to roll a crude cigarette, took a few hungry puffs, then regaining his voice, went on:

"I tore myself away from Irina, lifted her face between

my hands and kissed her lips—they were as cold as ice. I said good-bye to the children and ran to the train, jumping on to the steps as it was moving. It started off very slowly, and it took me past my family again. I looked at them and could see my orphaned kids huddling together, waving their hands and trying to smile, but not succeeding. And Irina stood there with her hands clasped to her chest, her lips white as chalk. She was whispering something and staring straight at me. Her body was bent forward as if she was trying to walk against a strong wind. And that's how she will live in my memory for the rest of my life. That's how I see her in my dreams, too. How could I push her away like that? Even now, when I think of it, it's like a knife twisting in my heart.

"We were assigned to our units at Belaya Tserkov, in the Ukraine. I was given a three-tonner, and that's what I drove in to the front. Well, it's no use telling you about the war. You were in it yourself and you know how it was. At the beginning I'd get a lot of letters from home, but I didn't write much myself. Just now and then I'd let them know that everything was all right and that I was doing some fighting. We may be retreating at present, I'd say, but it won't be long before we gather our strength and give the Fritzies something to remember us by. And what else was there to write? Those were sickening times and you didn't feel like writing. And I must say I was never the kind to whine. I couldn't stand the sight of those slobbering fools who wrote to their wives and kids every day whether there was anything to write about or not, just to rub their tears over the paper: 'Oh! it's such a tough life, oh! I might get killed.' And they'd run on like that, complaining and looking for sympathy, blubbering away. They didn't understand that those poor women and young ones were having just as bad a time of it back home. Why, the whole country rested on their shoulders. And what shoulders our women and children must have had not to give in under a weight like that!

79

But they didn't give in, they stuck it out! And then one of those weak sisters writes his sobby letter, and it just knocks his hard-working woman off her feet. After a letter like that, the poor thing is broken up and can't do her work. No! That's what a man's for, that's what it means to be a soldier —putting up with everything, enduring everything fate deals out. But if you're not man enough for that, then put on a skirt so you can look like a woman, at least from behind, and go and weed the beets, or milk the cows, because your kind aren't needed at the front. The stench is bad enough there without you.

"But I didn't get in even a year of fighting. I was wounded twice, but both times only slightly—once in the arm, the second time in the leg. The first was a bullet from a plane, the second a piece of shrapnel. And the Germans shot up my truck, top and sides, but I was lucky, friend. At first I was lucky all the time, and then my luck ran out. I got taken prisoner at Lozovenski, in May of 'forty-two. This is how it happened: The Germans were hitting hard and one of our 122-mm. howitzer batteries had nearly run out of ammunition. We piled my truck full of shells. I did the job myself, till my shirt stuck to my back. We had to hurry because they were closing in on us. From the left we could hear the tanks blasting away, and we heard firing from the right and in front. Things were getting real hot.

"'Do you think you can get through, Sokolov?' our company commander asked me. He needn't have asked. Was I going to sit around scratching myself while my comrades were getting killed? 'I've got to get through,' I said, 'that's all there's to it.' 'Then give it the works,' he said. And I stepped on the gas.

"I'd never driven like that in my life! I was aware that I wasn't carrying a load of potatoes. I knew I had to be careful with the stuff I had aboard, but how could I hold back when the men were fighting out there empty-handed, when the whole road was under artillery fire? I did about six kilometers and got pretty close to the place. I was about to turn off the road to get to the hollow where the battery was stationed, when what do I see? Our infantry running back across the field on both sides of the road, with the shells bursting all around them. What was I to do? I couldn't turn back, could I? So I gave her all she had. I was only about a kilometer from the battery. I had already turned off the road. But I never reached them, friend. A long-range gun must have dropped a big one near my truck. I never even heard the explosion or anything, just felt as if something cracked inside my head, and I didn't remember anything else. How I remained alive, and how long I lay there by the ditch, I have no idea. I came to but couldn't get up. My head kept jerking, I was shaking as from a bad chill, and I saw black. My left shoulder—there seemed to be something grinding inside it—and my body ached all over as if somebody had been hitting it for two days without a stop and with anything he could get hold of. I writhed on my belly for quite a while and finally managed to get up. But I still couldn't make out where I was, nor what had shaken me up that way. My memory was gone. I was afraid to lie down, I was afraid I'd pass out and never get up again. So I kept standing there, swaying like a poplar in a storm.

"When I came to and looked around, my heart felt as if someone had clamped it with a pair of pliers. The shells I'd been carrying were scattered all around me. Not far away was my truck, overturned, blown to bits, its wheels in the air. And the battle? The battle was going on behind me— just imagine that! When I realized what that meant, my legs folded under me and I fell as if I'd been cut down with an ax. I realized that I was surrounded by the enemy, that I was a prisoner of the fascists. That's war for you!

"No, brother, it's not an easy thing to understand, being taken prisoner through no fault of your own. It would take a lot of explaining, by one human being to another, especially to one who has not been through it himself, what it feels like.

"I lay there and soon heard the rumbling of tanks. Four medium German tanks went past at full speed in the direction I had come from with the ammunition. It was hard to bear the sight of them. Then came tow-cars hauling guns, and a mobile kitchen, then the infantry, not many of them, not more than a company. I looked at the Germans from the corner of my eye and then I pressed my face against the ground again, for it made me sick to look at them, sick at heart!

"When I thought they had all passed, I lifted my head, and there were six submachine-gunners marching along about a hundred feet away. And as I looked, they turned off the road and came straight toward me, all six of them, without saying a word. Well, I thought, there comes death. So I got into a sitting position. I didn't want to die lying down. Then I stood up. One of the Germans stopped a few feet away from me and jerked the gun from his shoulder. And, you know, man is a strange creature—at that moment I didn't feel any panic, not a shiver of fear moved my heart. I just looked at him and thought: 'He's going to make short shrift of me. I wonder where he'll shoot? At my head or across my chest?' As if it mattered a damn what part of my body he made his holes in.

"He was a young fellow, not badly built, dark-haired, but his lips were as thin as a thread, and his eyes had a mean look in them. 'That one will shoot me without giving it a thought,' I said to myself. And, sure enough, he raised his gun. I looked him straight in the eye and didn't say anything. But another one of them, a corporal or something, an older one, almost middle-aged, shouted something, pushed the other fellow aside, and came up to me. He jabbered something in his own language, and he bent my elbow feeling my muscle. 'O-o-oh!' he said, pointing along the road to where the sun was setting, as if to say: 'Off you go, you work horse, and toil for our Reich.' A thrifty type he was, he didn't like to waste anything.

"By then the dark-haired one had noticed my boots, they were a good pair. He pointed to them, saying: 'Take them off.' I sat down on the ground, took off my boots and handed them to him. He snatched them out of my hand. Then I unwound my foot-cloths and held them out to him, looking him up and down. He shouted and swore, and up went his gun again. The others stood there and roared with laughter. Then they marched off. The dark-haired one looked around at me about three times before we got to the road, and his eyes glittered with fury, like a wolf's. Why, anyone would have thought that I had taken his boots and not he mine.

"Well, brother, there was no getting away from them. I walked to the road, let out a most blood-curdling curse with all my Voronezh might, and turned to the west, a prisoner! As a walker I was right then good-for-nothing. I could do about a kilometer an hour, not more. I'd mean to place my foot in front of me, but somehow it would pull to the side, and swaying to and fro, I moved ahead like a drunkard. After a while a column of our men, from my own division, caught up with me. About ten German submachine-gunners were prodding them on. When the one at the head of the column came alongside of me, he struck me full force on the head with the butt of his gun, without saying a word. If I'd gone down, that would have been the end of me, he would have finished me off, but our men caught me as I was falling, shoved me into the middle, and for the next half hour carried me along, holding me up under my arms. And when I came to, one of them whispered: 'For God's sake don't fall down! Keep going or they'll kill you.' Although I had no strength at all left in me, I somehow managed to keep going.

"When the sun began to set, the Germans strengthened their guard. A truck delivered about another twenty sub-machine-gunners and they pushed us on at a faster pace. The men who were badly wounded could not keep up.

83

They were shot dead in the road. Two of the prisoners tried to run for it, not remembering that on a moonlit night you can see the very devil a mile off, and, of course, they were shot too.

"At about midnight we came to a half-burned village. They herded us into a church with a shattered cupola. The stone floor was bare, not a scrap of straw on it, and they had taken our heavy coats away from us. All they left on us were our tunics and trousers, so there was nothing to spread under us. Some of the men didn't even have their tunics on, just cotton undershirts. Most of these men were junior officers who had gotten rid of their tunics so that the Germans couldn't tell them from the rank and file soldiers. Those who had manned the artillery guns didn't have theirs on either, for they had been taken prisoner half-naked, while at their posts. A heavy rain came down during the night and we got soaked to the skin. Part of the roof had been blown off by a heavy shell, or a bomb from a plane, and the rest of it had been broken by shrapnel. You couldn't find a dry spot even at the altar. We crowded against each other all night like sheep in a dark pen.

"In the middle of the night I felt someone touch my arm, asking:

"'Comrade, are you wounded?'

"'Why do you want to know?' I replied—you couldn't trust just anyone.

"'I'm an army doctor, can I help you in any way?'

"I complained that my left shoulder snapped and creaked and was swollen and terribly painful.

"'Take off your tunic and undershirt,' he said sternly. I took them off and he began to poke his thin fingers around my shoulder so hard, that I saw stars. I gritted my teeth and said to him: 'You're a horse doctor, not a doctor for humans! Stop pressing where it hurts most, you heartless heathen.'

"But he kept on poking about and said, kind of angry,

'Your job is to keep quiet! Don't give me any trouble. Hold on, now it's really going to hurt.'

"And with these words he gave my arm such a wrench that red sparks flew from my eyes. When I got my senses back I asked him:

"'What do you think you're doing, you miserable fascist? My arm's broken into splinters and you give it a yank like that?'

"Then I heard him say, with a chuckle: 'I expected you to hit me with your right while I was pulling your left arm, but it seems you're a timid fellow. Your arm, however, was not broken, it was pulled out of joint, and I've just set it back. Does it feel better now?'

"Sure enough, I felt the pain leaving off. I thanked him from my heart, and he moved on in the darkness, asking in a whisper as he did so: 'Any wounded?'

"There was a real doctor for you! Even as a prisoner, and in pitch darkness, he went on doing good.

"In the morning they lined us up outside the church, a ring of submachine-gunners covering us. The SS officers began to pull out from among us those they thought most harmful to them. They asked who were Communists, who were officers, commissars, but no one admitted to being any of these. And there wasn't any traitor among us to give any of them away, nearly half of us were Communists, and there were many officers, too, and of course, commissars. But the SS did single out four from over two hundred of us—one Jew and three Russians from the rank and file. They picked out the Russians because they were dark-skinned and had wavy hair. They walked up to each of these three and asked: 'Jude?' The men said they were Russian, but the Germans didn't even listen, just said 'Step out,' and that was that.

"They shot all four, left the poor boys there, and drove us on farther."

III

"Since the day I was captured I'd been thinking of escaping. But I wanted to plan the thing right. All the way to Posnan, where they finally put us in a POW camp, I never got the right chance. But here, at Posnan, it looked as though I had found what I wanted. At the end of May, they sent several of us out to a little wood near the camp to dig graves for our comrades—many of our men kept dying from illness. So I kept digging away at the cursed Posnan clay and looking around me. I noticed that two of our guards had sat down some distance away to have a bite, while the third dozed off in the sun. So I put down my shovel and went quickly behind a bush. Then I ran for it, keeping straight toward the rising sun.

"It took the guards some time to realize that I was gone. Where I got the strength, all skin-and-bones that I was, to cover almost forty kilometers each day, I myself don't know. But nothing came of my dreams! On the fourth day, when I was already quite a distance from the camp, they caught me.

"They had put bloodhounds on my trail, and they found me in an unharvested field of oats. At dawn on that fourth day, I had reached an open field, and there were about three kilometers to the next wood. Fearing to cross to it in daytime, I decided to hide in the oats till dark. I crushed some of the grain in my hand and was filling my pockets with a supply when I heard the yelping of dogs and the rattle of motorcycles. My heart sank. The barking was getting closer. I lay flat and covered my head with my arms so the hounds couldn't get at my face. They were soon on top of me and it took them about a minute to tear all the rags off me. They left me in what I was born in. They dragged me through the oats and did as they liked with me, and in the end one of them, a huge one, got his forepaws on my chest, aimed his snout at my throat, but paused for his masters.

"The Germans drove up on two motorcycles. They beat me up, as only those beasts could beat a man, and then they set the dogs on me again. I was taken back to camp naked and bloody as I was, and was thrown into solitary for a month. But I was still alive—and somehow stayed alive.

"It hurts, brother, to remember all this, and even more to talk about it, about what we had to bear as prisoners. When I remember the inhuman treatment we suffered there, in Germany, when I think of all my fellow countrymen who died of torture there, in the camps, it grips my heart and I can hardly breathe.

"Where didn't they shove me in those two years I was a prisoner! Half of Germany I trudged through in that time, from camp to camp. I was in Saxony working at a silicate plant, in the Ruhr hauling coal, in Bavaria breaking my back over their fields, in Thüringen, and the devil only knows over what other German soil I didn't drag myself. Nature over there is varied, no two places seem the same, but, brother, no matter where we were, they beat and shot our men in the same way. Those skunks and parasites beat us like no man here ever beat an animal. They pounded us with their fists, stamped on us with their feet, went at us with rubber truncheons and with any piece of iron they could lay their hands on, not to mention their rifle butts and other weapons.

"They beat you because you were a Russian, because you were still alive and seeing the light of this world, because you worked for them—the swine. They beat you because they didn't like the way you looked at them or how you walked when you turned. They beat you so as to knock the very life out of you.

"And everywhere we went they fed us in the same way, five ounces of ersatz bread made half out of sawdust, and a thin swill with turnips. In some places they gave us hot water to drink and in others they didn't. But what's the use of talking—judge for yourself. In the summer, before the war started, I weighed over two hundred pounds and by the autumn I couldn't have weighed more than one hundred twenty. Just skin and bones and not enough strength to carry the bones around. But they made you work, and you couldn't say a word, and the work we were made to do would have killed a dray-horse.

"At the beginning of September they transferred a hundred and fifty of us POWs from a camp near Kustrin to Camp B-14, not far from Dresden. Together with this hundred and fifty there were about two thousand in this camp. We were all working in a stone quarry, cutting and crushing the German stone with only hand tools. The minimum was four cubic meters a day for each man, and for a man, mind you, who was keeping his body and soul together by a slender thread. And it was there things really got bad. Within two months, out of the hundred and fifty men transferred there, only fifty-seven were left. We barely had time to bury our dead, and added to all that was the rumor in the camp that the Fritzes had taken Stalingrad and were pushing on into Siberia. One blow was piled on top of another. And they had us beaten down so that we couldn't lift our eyes from the ground. We looked like beggars asking to be interred in their German earth. But the camp guards were giddy with triumph and day after day kept drinking, belting out their songs, celebrating.

"One evening, we returned to the prisoners' hut from work, soaked to the bone. It had rained all day. We were shivering from the cold so that we couldn't keep our teeth from chattering. There was no place to dry off or get warmed up, and we were hungry as death, maybe even hungrier. We were never given food in the evenings.

"Well, I peeled off my soaking rags, threw them on my bunk, saying: 'They want you to do four cubic meters a day, but one cubic meter would be plenty to bury you in.' That was what I said. Would you believe it, there was a dirty dog in our midst who reported to the commandant my bitter words.

"Our camp commandant, or *Lagerführer*, as they were called, was named Müller. He wasn't tall, but thick-set, tow-headed, and sort of bleached all over, the hair on his head, his eyebrows, eyelashes, even his bulging eyes were whitish. He spoke Russian as well as you and I. He even talked like a native of the Volga region, with their kind of full, rounded O in his speech. And was he a master at swearing! Where he learned to swear like that in Russian only the devil knows. He'd line us up in front of the block—that's what they called the prisoners' huts—and walk down the line sur-rounded by his pack of SS men, his right hand at the ready, and he would bloody every other man's nose for him—'preventative for the flu' he would call it. Altogether there were four blocks in the camp and each day he'd give the men from a different block their 'preventative for the flu.' And that industrious dog never took a day off. There was one thing, however, that he didn't realize. Before he would go through that routine, he would stand there in front of us men and work himself up by swearing for all he was worth. And this made us feel a little better. You see, the words sounded familiar, they were like a breath of air from back home. If he'd understood that his cursing gave us some pleasure, I suppose he wouldn't have done it in Russian, but in his own tongue. One of my pals, a Moscovite, would get livid. 'When he curses,' he'd say to me, 'I shut my eyes, make believe I'm back in Moscow having one with the boys, and I get so thirsty for a glass of beer, my head begins to spin.'

"Well, the day after I said that about the cubic meters, this same commandant called me to account. That evening an interpreter and two guards came for me.

"'Sokolov, Andrei?'

"I answered.

" 'Follow us. On the double! The *Herr Lagerführer* wants to see you.'

"I knew why he sent for me. To put an end to me, that's why, for saying those words. So I took leave of my comrades—they all knew I was going to my death—took a deep breath, and left with the guards. Walking across the camp yard I looked up at the stars, said good-bye to them too, and thought to myself: 'You've had your share of torment, Andrei Sokolov, POW Number 331.' I felt sorry for Irina and the kids, then the pity for them lessened in me, and I began to screw up my courage so that I could face the barrel of that revolver without flinching, as befits a soldier, so that the enemy would not see how hard it was for me, in the last moments of my life, to part with it.

"There were flowers on the window sill in the commandant's room. It was nice and clean there, like in one of our clubrooms at home. At the table sat the full staff of officers. The five of them sat there downing schnapps and chewing bacon fat. On the table there was a big, open bottle of schnapps, bread, bacon, pickled apples, and all kinds of cans of food. I glanced at all that grub and you wouldn't believe it, I felt sick to my stomach. Always hungry as a wolf, I had forgotten what human food looked like, and now all this abundance before my eyes! I controlled my nausea, but it took a great effort to tear my eyes away from that table.

"Right in front of me sat the half-drunk Müller, playing with his pistol, throwing it with one hand and catching it with the other. He had his eyes fixed on me, never blinking, just like a snake. Well, I stood at attention, snapped my broken-down heels together, and reported in a loud voice:

" 'Prisoner of war Andrei Sokolov, at your service, Herr Kommandant.'

"And he asks me: 'Russian Ivan, is four cubic meters of quarrying too much for you?'

" 'Yes, Herr Kommandant,' I said, 'it's too much.'

"'And will one cubic meter be enough for your grave?'

"'Yes, Herr Kommandant, quite enough and some to spare.'

"He then got up and said: 'I'll now do you the great honor of shooting you, in person, for those words. You'll make a mess here, let's go out into the yard. You can sign off there.'

"'As you wish,' I said to him.

"He stood there, thought for a minute, threw his pistol on the table, poured out a full glass of schnapps, took a piece of bread, put a slice of bacon on it, and offered it all to me, saying:

"'Before you die, Russian Ivan, drink to the victory of German arms.'

"I was about to take the glass and the bread from his hands, but when I heard those words, something set me on fire inside. I thought to myself: 'Me, a Russian soldier, drink to the triumph of German arms? What will you ask next, Herr Kommandant? Let the devil take me, but you can go to hell with your schnapps!'

"I took the glass and the bread from him and put them on the table, saying:

"'Thank you for your hospitality, but I'm not a drinking man.'

"He smiled: 'So you won't drink to our victory? In that case, drink to your own death.'

"What could I lose? 'To my own death and relief from torture, I'll drink,' I said to him, lifted the glass and poured the stuff down my throat in two gulps. But the bread I didn't touch. I just wiped my lips politely with my hand and said:

"'Thank you for your hospitality. I'm ready, Herr Kommandant. You can put an end to me now.'

"But he looked at me sharply, and said:

"'Go ahead, have a bite to eat before you die.'

"And I answered:

"'I never eat after the first drink.'

"He poured out a second glass and handed it to me. I drank it and again didn't touch the food. I was staking everything on courage. Anyway, I thought, I might as well get drunk before I go out into that yard to part with my life.

"The commandant raised his eyebrows high and asked: 'Why don't you eat, Russian Ivan? Don't be bashful.'

"But I stuck to my guns: 'Forgive me, Herr Kommandant, but I never eat after the second glass either.'

"He puffed out his cheeks and snorted and then roared with laughter, saying something rapidly in German—he must have been translating what I said to his buddies. The others laughed too, fidgeted in their chairs, turned their big mugs around to stare at me, and I noticed something different in the way they looked at me, something a little human.

"The commandant poured out a third glass, and his hands were shaking as he laughed. I drank that glass slowly, bit off a little bit of the bread, and put the rest down on the table. I wanted to show the swine that even though I was perishing from hunger, I wasn't going to gobble up the scraps they threw to me, that I still had my Russian dignity and pride, and that they had not turned me into a beast, though they had tried hard enough.

"After that the commandant got a solemn look on his face, adjusted the two iron crosses on his chest, came out from behind the table unarmed, and said:

"'You know what, Sokolov? You're a real Russian soldier. You're a brave soldier. I'm a soldier, too, and I respect a worthy enemy. I won't shoot you. I want you to know that today our valiant troops reached the Volga and took complete possession of your Stalingrad. This is a great day for us, and because of that I magnanimously spare you your life. Go back to your block and take this with you for your courage.'

"And he handed me a small loaf of bread from the table and a slab of bacon. I clutched that bread to my chest as tightly as I could, and picked up the bacon with my other hand. I was so overcome by this unexpected turn of events that I even forgot to say thank you, did a left turn, went to the door, and all that time I was thinking to myself: 'Now he'll blast me from behind, between my shoulder blades, and I'll never make it to the hut with this food for my comrades. But nothing happened. Again death passed me by, letting me feel only a good whiff of its cold breath.

"I got out of the commandant's room without staggering, but outside I went reeling all over the place. I swayed into the barracks, fell flat on the cement floor, and passed out.

"The men woke me next morning when it was still dark. They wanted to know what had happened. I remembered every detail of what had taken place at the commandant's and told them the whole story.

"'How are we going to divide the food?' the man in the bunk next to me asked, his voice trembling.

"'Equal shares all around,' I said.

"We waited till it got light. We cut up the bread and the bacon fat with a piece of thread. Each of us got a piece of bread about the size of a matchbox, taking every crumb into account. As for the fat, well, there was, of course, enough only to grease your lips with. But no one was cheated out of that either."

IV

"Soon after that day they sent off about three hundred of the strongest of us to drain marshes, then we went to the Ruhr to work in the mines. And there I remained until 'forty-four. By then our Army had knocked some of the stuffings out of the Germans, and the fascists stopped treating us prisoners as though we were the scum of the earth. One day they lined us up, the whole day shift, and some visiting *Oberlieutenant* said, through an interpreter:

"'Any one who had served in the army or had worked before the war as a driver—step out.'

"About seven of us stepped forward. They gave us some worn overalls, and took us under guard to Potsdam. When we got there, they separated us. I was detailed to Todt. That was what they called the outfit for building roads and defense installations.

"I was assigned to drive a German army engineer, a major, around in an Opel-Admiral. There was a fascist hog for you! He was a short one, with a pot-belly, he was as wide as he was tall, and had a rear like a bass drum. Three chins hung over his collar, and in the back there were three folds of fat around his neck. He must have had at least two hundred pounds of pure fat on him. When he moved he puffed like a steam engine, and when he sat down to eat—you never saw anything like it! He'd go on munching all day and taking swigs from his flask. Now and then I got a bit of it, too. He'd stop on the road, slice up some sausage and cheese, and chase it down with some of the whisky, and when he was in a good mood he'd throw me a piece, like to a dog. He never handed it to me, considered that beneath him. But, just the same, my new life was a good deal better than at the POW camp. I gradually began to resemble a human being, and I even began to put on some weight.

"For about two weeks I drove the major from Potsdam to Berlin, and back. Then they sent him closer to the front-line area, to supervise the building of fortifications against our troops. It was then that I began to lose some sleep. Night after night I'd think of how to escape to our side, to my own country.

"One day we drove to the town of Polotsk. There, at dawn, I heard, for the first time in two years, the rumble of our artillery, and, brother, you can't imagine how my heart thumped at that sound! I tell you, friend, not even when I first began to court Irina did it ever beat like that! There was fighting going on east of Polotsk, about eighteen kilometers away. The Germans were mad and jumpy, and my old pot-belly started drinking more and more. During the day I would drive him around and he'd give out instructions about those fortifications, and at night he'd sit by himself, drinking. He grew all puffy and there were huge bags under his eyes.

"Well, I soon decided there was no need to wait any longer, that my hour had come, and that I wasn't going to escape by myself. I made up my mind to take along old pot-belly. I knew he'd be useful to our cause.

"I found a five-pound weight in some ruins and wound a rag around it, so that if I had to hit him, there wouldn't be any blood. I picked up a length of telephone wire in the road, got everything ready that I might need, and hid it all under the front seat of the Opel. One evening, two days before I said good-bye to the Germans, I was on my way back from the filling station, when I saw a German soldier staggering along dead drunk, groping along the wall. I pulled up, led him into a bombed building, shook him out of his uniform, and took his cap off his head. These things, too, I hid under the seat. So, there I was, all set.

"On the morning of June 29th, my major told me to take him out of town in the direction of Trosnitsa. He had a job to do there. We drove off. He installed himself in the back seat, and was soon asleep, and I sat in front, my heart almost jumping out of my mouth. I drove fast but slowed down very gradually outside the town, in order not to wake the major, then stopped, got out, and looked around. At some distance behind, two trucks were slowly coming our way. I pulled out my iron weight and opened the door wide. Old pot-belly was lying back on the seat snoring away. Well, I gave him one on the left temple with the weight. His head flopped on to his chest. I gave him another one, just to make sure, but I didn't want to kill him. I was determined to deliver him alive, for he was going to be able to tell our men a lot of things they wanted to know. I pulled the pistol out of his holster and shoved it into my pocket. Then I pushed a bracket down behind the back seat, tied the telephone wire around the major's neck, and fastened it to the bracket. That was so he wouldn't fall over on his side when I drove fast, or fall off the seat. I pulled on the German uniform and cap. Then I drove the car straight for the place where the earth was rumbling, where the fighting was.

"I roared across the German front line between two pillboxes. A pack of machine-gunners popped up out of a dugout and I slowed down so they would see I had a major with me. They shouted and waved their arms to tell me I mustn't go on, but I pretended not to understand, stepped on the gas, and took off at about eighty. Before they realized what was happening and opened fire, I was in no-man's-land, weaving around the shellholes like a hare gone mad.

"There were the Germans, firing from behind, and there were our boys, as if possessed, giving it to me hard from the front. They put their bullets through the windshield and riddled the radiator. But not far away I spotted a small wood by a lake, and some of our soldiers running toward the car, so I made it into that wood, opened the door, fell to the ground, kissed it, hardly able to breathe in that sweet Russian air.

"A young fellow with some kind of khaki shoulder straps on his tunic I'd never seen before, got to me first and said with a scowl: 'Aha, you Fritzy devil, lost your way, eh?' I tore off the German uniform, threw the cap at my feet, and said to him: 'Boy, you're a sight for sore eyes! You beautiful creature! Are you calling *me* a Fritz? Me who was born and bred in Voronezh! I was a prisoner of war, now do you get it? Come on, untie that fat hog sitting in the car, take his briefcase, and escort me to your commander.'

"I handed over my pistol and was passed from one to another until, toward evening, I found myself before the colonel in command of the division. By that time I had been fed, taken to the bathhouse, questioned, and given a new uniform. I appeared before the colonel in good shape, clean in body and soul, and in full uniform. He got up from his table and came over to greet me, and in front of all the officers he put his arms around me and said:

"'Thank you, soldier, for the fine present you brought us from the Germans. Your major and his briefcase are more valuable to us than any twenty Germans we might have questioned. I'll recommend you for a military decoration!'

"And I, moved by his words and the affection he showed me, could hardly keep my lips from trembling, and all I could say was: 'I beg you, comrade colonel, to enroll me in an infantry unit.'

"The colonel laughed, clapped me on the shoulder, and said, 'What kind of a fighter do you think you'd make when you can hardly stand on your feet? I'm sending you off to a hospital right now. They'll patch you up and fatten you up, after that you'll get a month's leave to go home to your family, and when you come back, we'll see what we'll do with you.'

"The colonel and all the officers in the dugout said good-bye to me, each shaking my hand, and I left feeling completely unhinged, because in the two years I had been prisoner I got so unused to human treatment. I can tell you, brother, it was a long time before I stopped drawing my head into my shoulders when talking to a superior, from the habit of being afraid I might be struck. That's the kind of habits we picked up in the fascist camps.

"I wrote to Irina as soon as I got to the hospital. I told her briefly about having been a prisoner of war and about the escape with the German major. And, maybe *you* can tell me, why I boasted in this letter, like a kid? I couldn't even keep from telling her that the colonel promised to recommend me for a medal.

"Then I did nothing but eat and sleep for two whole weeks. They fed me a little at a time, but often, otherwise if they had given me all the food I craved, the doctor said, I'd have gotten good and sick. At the end of the two weeks

I couldn't swallow another mouthful. There had been no answer from home and I must say I began to feel very uneasy. I couldn't even think of eating and couldn't sleep, and all sorts of black thoughts kept creeping into my head. During the third week, I got a letter from Voronezh. It wasn't from Irina, but from a neighbor of ours, the carpenter Ivan Timofeevich. God grant that no one else ever receive such a letter! He informed me that way back in June of 'forty-two the Germans bombed the aircraft factory, and that my home was demolished by a direct hit from a heavy bomb. Irina and the girls were at home when it happened. And he wrote that not a trace was found of them, just a deep crater where the house had been. I couldn't go on reading—everything went dark before me and my heart tightened into such a knot that I thought it would never loosen up again. I lay back on my cot to get some strength back, then I read to the end. My neighbor also wrote that Anatoly, my son, was away in town during the raid. He returned in the evening, saw the crater where his home had been and went back to the city that same night. Before leaving he told my neighbor that he was volunteering for the front.

"When my heart eased up and I could think once more, I remembered how forlorn my Irina had been when we parted at the station. Her woman's heart must have known even then that we'd never see each other again. And I had pushed her away. . . . So, I had a family once, a home, it had all taken years to come by, and it was all destroyed in a flash. I was now alone. And I thought: 'This isn't real, I must be dreaming about this shattered life of mine!' When I was a prisoner I'd talk to Irina and the kids nearly every night, to myself of course, trying to cheer them up, telling them I'd come home, and not to cry. 'I'm tough, I'd say to them, I'll survive, we'd surely be together again some day. . . .'

"For those two years I had been talking to the dead!"

The man was silent for a moment, and when he spoke

again, his voice was low and it faltered. "Let's have a smoke, friend. Grief is choking me."

V

We lighted up. In the flooded woodland the woodpecker's tapping rang very loud. The warm breeze still rustled lazily the dry catkins on the alders, the clouds were still floating in the sky's blueness as though under taut white sails. But in those moments of sorrowful silence, the world getting ready for the great fulfillment of spring, for its eternal affirmation of life, seemed quite different to me now.

It was painful to keep silent, and I asked: "What happened then?"

"Then?" the storyteller said reluctantly. "Then I got a month's leave, and a week later I was in Voronezh. I went on foot to the place where I had once lived as a family man. There was a deep crater full of rusty water and all around it the weeds were waist high. The place was deserted, sunk in a graveyard stillness. I tell you, brother, it was more than a man could bear. I stood there for a while, giving in to my grief, then I went back to the station. I couldn't stand to be there for more than an hour. I returned to the division the same day.

"About three months later a ray of joy shone even on me. I heard from Anatoly. My son wrote me from another front. He had got my address from the neighbor, that same Ivan Timofeevich. He wrote me he'd been to an artillery school at first; his gift for mathematics had come in handy. Within a year he graduated with honors and was sent to the front as a captain, and he was now commanding a battery, and had won six orders and medals. It was plain he had outdone his old man in everything! Once more I felt real proud of him! It was no small thing—my own son a captain and in charge of a battery. It was something to be proud of! And all those decorations, too. It didn't bother me that his father was just hauling shells and other such military stuff about in

101

a Studebaker. His father's time was past, but for him, so young and already a captain, everything lay ahead.

"And nights I had begun to have an elderly man's dreams. When the war was over, I'd get my son married, settle down near the young couple, do a bit of carpentry, and look after their kids—you know, the kind of things an aging man does. But that, too, misfired. In the winter we kept advancing without stopping to catch our breath, and there wasn't time to write to each other often, but toward the end of the war, when our army was near Berlin, I sent Anatoly a letter one morning. And I got an answer the very next day. I found out that he and I had advanced up to the German capital by different routes and were now close to each other. I could hardly wait for the moment when we'd meet. Well, the moment came. . . . Exactly on the 9th of May, on the morning of Victory Day, a German sniper killed my Anatoly.

"The company commander had sent for me in the afternoon. I noticed a strange artillery officer sitting there. When I came into the room this officer stood up as if he was meeting a senior in rank. My commanding officer said:

"'He's here to see you, Sokolov,' and turned away to the window.

"Something went through me like an electric shock. I knew there was trouble. The lieutenant colonel came up to me and said:

"'Bear up, father. Your son, Captain Sokolov, was killed today at his battery. Come with me.'

"I swayed, but kept on my feet. Even now, it still seems unreal the way the lieutenant colonel and I drove in that big car along those streets strewn with rubble, and I remember, as if through a fog, the soldiers drawn up in a line at the coffin covered with red velvet.

"But Anatoly I still see as plainly as I see you now, friend. I went up to the coffin. Yes, it was my son lying there, and yet it wasn't. My son had been a boy, always smiling, with narrow shoulders and a sharp little Adam's apple sticking out of his thin neck. But here was a young, broad-shouldered, good-looking man. His eyes were half-closed as if he was looking past me into some unknown, distant place. Only at the corners of his lips showed a bit of the smile of my former son, the Anatoly I once knew. I kissed him and stepped aside. The lieutenant colonel made a speech. My Anatoly's friends were wiping their tears, but my unshed tears must have dried up in my heart. Maybe that's why it still hurts so much.

"I buried my last joy and hope in that alien German soil! The battery fired a volley to send off their commander on his long journey, and something seemed to snap inside me. When I got back to my unit I was a changed man. Soon after that, I was demobilized. Where was I to go? To Voronezh? Couldn't stand even to think of it! I remembered I had a friend who had been discharged from the Army the previous winter and was living in Uruypinsk. He had asked me once to come and live with him. So I went.

"My friend and his wife had no children and lived in a cottage of their own on the edge of town. He had a disability pension but worked as a driver in a trucking depot, so I got a job there, too. I moved in with my friend, and they made a home for me. We used to deliver loads in the suburbs, and in the autumn we switched over to grain delivery work. It was then that I met my new son, the one that's playing down there in the sand.

"First thing I'd do when I'd get back from a long haul would be to go to a café for a bite and, of course, I'd have a glass of vodka to pick me up. It was a bad habit, but I must say I had quite a liking for the stuff by that time. Well, one day I saw this little boy near the café, and the next day I noticed him again. What a little bag of rags he was. His face was all smeared with watermelon juice and dust, the dirt on him was an inch thick, his hair was a mess, but his eyes were like the stars at night after a rain! And I got so fond of him that, strange as it may seem, I began to

103

miss him, and I'd hurry to finish my work so I could get back to the café and see him sooner. That's where he'd get his food—ate whatever people happened to give him.

"On the fourth day, I drove up to the café straight from the state farm, with my truckload of grain. There was the little fellow sitting on the steps, kicking his legs, and looking quite hungry. I stuck my head out of the window and called to him: 'Hey, Vanyushka! Come on, get in, I'll take you to the elevator with me, then we'll come back here and have some food.'

"My voice made him start, then he jumped from the steps, scrambled up to the high running board, and pulled himself up to the window, saying softly: 'How do you know that my name is Vanya?' and he opened those eyes of his wide, waiting for my answer. Well, I told him I was one of those guys who's been around and knew everything. He then came running to the right side. I opened the door, sat him down beside me, and off we went. He was a lively one, but he suddenly got quiet and thoughtful, stared at me from under his long curly eyelashes, then sighed. Such a little one, but he had already learned to sigh! Was that a thing for such a young one to be doing?

" 'Where's your father, Vanya?' I asked.

" 'He was killed at the front,' he said in a whisper.

" 'And Mommie?'

" 'Mommie was killed by a bomb when we were on the train.'

" 'Where were you coming from on the train?'

" 'I don't know, I can't remember. . . .'

" 'And haven't you got any family at all?'

" 'No, nobody.'

" 'But where do you sleep at night?'

" 'Anywhere I can find.'

"I felt the hot tears welling up inside me and I made up my mind right then: We are not going to perish in solitude, each one of us all alone in the world! I'll take him in as my child. And right away I felt easier and there was a sort of brightness inside of me. I leaned over to him and asked, very quietly: 'Vanya, do you know who I am?'

"And he sort of breathed it out: 'Who?'

"And still as quietly, I said to him: 'I—am your father.'

"My God, what happened then! He threw his arms around my neck, kissed my cheeks, my lips, my forehead, and in a ringing little voice, chirped away like a canary: 'Daddy, my own dear daddy! I've been waiting for you to find me!'

"He pressed against me, trembling all over like a blade of grass in the breeze. My eyes were wet and I was trembling too, and my hands shook. How I managed to hold on to the wheel at all, I don't know. Even so, we landed in the ditch, and I stopped the engine. While my eyes were moist I was afraid to drive for fear I'd knock someone down. We stopped for about five minutes, and my little son kept clinging to me with all his little might, not saying anything, just trembling all over. I put my right arm around him, hugged him gently, turned the truck around with my left hand, and drove home with him. I didn't feel up to going to the grain elevator after that 'reunion.'

"I parked the truck at the gate, took my new son in my arms, and carried him into my friend's cottage. Vanya put his arms around my neck and hung on tight. He pressed his face to my unshaven cheek and stuck there as if glued to me. And that's how I carried him in. My friend and his wife happened to be at home. I came in and winked at them with both eyes. Then said loudly and cheerfully: 'Look, I've found my little Vanya, at last! Welcome us, good people!'

"They hadn't had any children themselves, but they guessed at once what was up and started bustling about. And I just couldn't get my son away from me. But I managed somehow to convince him that I'd not disappear again. I washed his hands with soap and sat him down at the table. My friend's wife gave him a plate of soup, and when she saw how hungrily he gulped it down, she just burst into

105

tears. She stood there at the stove crying into her apron. And my Vanya, seeing her cry, ran up to her, tugged at her skirt, and said: 'Why are you crying? My daddy found me at the café, you should be glad, and you're crying.' This made her cry all the more.

"After dinner I took him to the barber's to have his hair cut, and at home I gave him a bath in a wooden tub, and wrapped him up in a clean sheet. He put his arms around me and fell asleep in my lap. I laid him gently on the bed, drove off to the elevator, unloaded the grain, and took the truck to the garage. Then I went to the stores. I bought him a pair of woolen pants, a little shirt, a pair of sandals, and a straw cap. Of course, they were all the wrong size and of poor quality. My friend's wife even gave me a scolding for those pants. 'Are you crazy,' she said, 'dressing a boy in wool in heat like this?!' And the next minute she had her sewing machine on the table and was rummaging in the trunk. In an hour she had a pair of polished cotton shorts and a little white short-sleeved shirt ready for my Vanyushka.

"I took him to bed with me that evening and for the first time in many a night I fell asleep peacefully. I woke up about four times though. And there he was, nestling in the crook of my arm, like a sparrow under the eaves, snuffing softly. I can't find words to tell you how much delight I felt just at the sight of him. I'd try to lie still, so as not to wake him, but I just couldn't. I'd get up very quietly, light a match, and stand there feasting my eyes on him.

"Just before daybreak I woke. I couldn't make out why it had become so hard to breathe in the room. It was my little son—he'd climbed out of his sheet and was lying right across my chest, with his little foot against my throat. He's a fidgety sleeper, but I've got used to him, and miss him when he is not at my side. At night I can look at him while he's asleep, I can smell his curls, and it takes some of the pain out of my heart, helps it feel again. You see, it had just about turned to stone.

"At first he used to ride with me on the truck, then I decided that that had to stop. After all, I didn't need much when I was on my own. A piece of bread and an onion with a pinch of salt would last a soldier a whole day. But with him it was different. Now I'd have to get him some milk, or go home and cook an egg for him, and he had to have something hot to eat. So I had to attend to my work and earn well. I got up my courage and left him in the care of my friend's wife. He cried all day and in the evening ran away to the elevator to find me. Waited there till late at night.

"I had a hard time with him at first. Once, after a very hard day at work, we went to bed when it was still light. He'd always chatter like a sparrow, but this time he was very quiet. 'What's on your mind, sonny?' I asked. He looked up at the ceiling, and said, 'What did you do with your leather coat, Daddy?' Me, I'd never had a leather coat in my life! So, I had to think fast.

" 'Left it in Voronezh,' I told him.

" 'And why did it take you so long to find me?'

" 'I looked for you, my son, in Germany, in Poland, and all over Byelorussia, and you turned up in Uryupinsk.'

" 'Is Uryupinsk nearer than Germany? Is it far from our house to Poland?'

"This is the way we went on talking till we dropped off to sleep. Perhaps you think, friend, there wasn't a reason for his asking about that leather coat? No, there was a reason behind it all right. It meant that at some time or other Vanya's real father had worn a coat like that, and that he had later remembered it. A child's memory is like summer lightning, it flashes and lights things up for a moment, then disappears. And that was how Vanyushka's memory worked, like those flashes of lightning.

"We might have gone on living there another year, in Uryupinsk, but in November I had an accident. I was driving along a muddy village road and skidded. A cow got in the way and I knocked her over. Well, you know how that

107

is—the women raised a fuss, a crowd gathered, and soon the traffic inspector was there. He took my license away although I begged him to be easy on me. The cow had got up, had stuck its tail in the air and stomped off through the alleys, but I lost my license. I worked through the rest of the winter as a carpenter, then got in touch with an old army friend in Kashary, and he invited me to come and stay with him. He told me I could do carpenter's work there, then get a new license in his region. So now my son and I are making the trip to Kashary—on foot.

"But, I tell you, even if I hadn't had that accident with the cow, I'd have left Uryupinsk just the same. My memories don't give me peace, I can't stay in one place for long. When my Vanyushka gets older and has to be enrolled in a school, I suppose I'll give in and settle down somewhere. But for the time being the two of us are roaming the Russian land together."

"Isn't it hard on him?" I asked.

"No, he doesn't go far on his own two feet. Most of the time he rides on me. I lift him on to my shoulder and carry him, and when he wants to move about he jumps down and runs around at the side of the road, prancing like a little goat. No, brother, it's not that that worries me, we'd make it all right. The trouble is my heart's got a knock in it somewhere, I guess I ought to have a piston changed. Sometimes it gives me such a stab that I see black. I'm afraid that one day I may die in my sleep, and frighten my little son. And there's this other thing—nearly every night I see in my sleep the dear ones who have died. And it's as if I am behind barbed wire and they are on the other side, and free. I talk to Irina and the children about all kinds of things, but as soon as I try to push aside the barbed wire, they fade away before my eyes. And it's odd, in the daytime I always keep a firm grip on myself, you'll never hear me sigh or moan, but there are times when I wake up at night and my pillow is wet through with tears."

The sound of my friend's voice and the splash of oars echoed in the forest.

This stranger, who now seemed my close friend, held out his large hand, hard as wood:

"Good-bye, brother, good luck to you!"

"Good luck, and a good journey to Kashary!"

"I thank you. Come, sonny, let's go to the boat."

The boy ran to his father's side, took hold of the corner of his padded jacket, and started off with tiny steps beside the striding man.

Two orphaned creatures, two grains of sand, swept into strange parts by the force of the hurricane of war. . . . What did the future hold for them? I wanted to believe that this Russian man, a man of unbreakable will, would win out, and that the boy would grow at his side into a man who could endure anything, overcome any obstacle.

I felt sad as I watched them go. Perhaps everything would have been all right at our parting but for Vanyushka. After he had gone a few steps, he twisted around on his short little legs and waved to me with his tiny pink hand. And then something clawed at my heart, and I quickly turned away. No, not only in our sleep do we weep, we, the middle-aged men whose hair grew gray in the years of war. We weep, too, in our waking hours. The important thing is to be able to turn away in time. The most important thing is not to wound a child's heart, not to let him see the unwilling hot tear that runs down the cheek of a man.

1957

Except for three years spent in Moscow in his youth, MIKHAIL SHO-LOKHOV has lived in the same Russian village on the Don where he was born in 1905. As a boy he attended parochial school and high school, but his education was interrupted by the Russian Revolution of 1917, and he never resumed his studies.

After fighting with the Red forces in the Civil War for four years, he began to write, and had his first story published in 1924. His novel, *And Quiet Flows the Don,* for which, in 1965, he was awarded the Nobel Prize for Literature, took ten years in the writing.

Sholokhov's name is known wherever books are published and read. His works have been published outside Russia in over two hundred editions and in more than thirty languages, including Urdu, Malayan, and Turkish.

MIRIAM MORTON was born in Russia, which partially accounts for her deep and sympathetic understanding of the characters in Sholokhov's stories. She has been called a "superb" translator by *The Saturday Review,* and reviewers in other publications have judged her translations "excellent," "masterly," "remarkable," and "splendid."

Mrs. Morton is the first American translator of Sholokhov; other translators of his work have been British.

As a young girl, she came to this country with her family, and became a citizen in her adolescence.